a

Woman.

INTRODUCING
PAGES & PRIVILEGES™.

It's our way of thanking you for buying
our books at your favorite retail store.

GET ALL THIS FREE

WITH JUST ONE PROOF OF PURCHASE:

◆ **Hotel Discounts** up
to 60% at home and
abroad ◆ **Travel Service**
- Guaranteed lowest
published airfares
plus 5% cash back
on tickets ◆ **$25 Travel Voucher**
◆ **Sensuous Petite Parfumerie** collection

$50 VALUE

◆ **Insider Tips Letter**
with sneak previews
of upcoming books

*You'll get a FREE personal card, too.
It's your passport to all these benefits— and to
even more great gifts & benefits to come!*

There's no club to join. No purchase commitment. No obligation.

MW01110387

Enrollment Form

☐ *Yes!* I WANT TO BE A *PRIVILEGED WOMAN.*

Enclosed is one *PAGES & PRIVILEGES™* Proof of Purchase
from any Harlequin or Silhouette book currently for
sale in stores (Proofs of Purchase are found on
the back pages of books) and the store cash
register receipt. Please enroll me in *PAGES
& PRIVILEGES™.* Send my Welcome
Kit and FREE Gifts -- and activate my
FREE benefits -- immediately.

*More great gifts and benefits to come like these
luxurious Truly Lace and L'Effleur gift baskets.*

NAME (please print)
_____

ADDRESS _____ APT. NO _____

CITY _____ STATE _____ ZIP/POSTAL CODE _____

📖 PROOF OF PURCHASE SAMPLE ONLY	**NO CLUB!** **NO COMMITMENT!** *Just one purchase brings you great **Free Gifts** and **Benefits!***

Please allow 6-8 weeks for delivery. Quantities are
limited. We reserve the right to substitute items.
Enroll before October 31, 1995 and receive
one full year of benefits.

(More details in back of this book.)

Name of store where this book was purchased_____

Date of purchase_____

Type of store:

☐ Bookstore   ☐ Supermarket   ☐ Drugstore

☐ Dept. or discount store (e.g. K-Mart or Walmart)

☐ Other (specify)_____

Which Harlequin or Silhouette series do you usually read?

Complete and mail with one Proof of Purchase and store receipt to:

U.S.: *PAGES & PRIVILEGES™,* P.O. Box 1960, Danbury, CT 06813-1960

Canada: *PAGES & PRIVILEGES™,* 49-6A The Donway West, P.O. 813,
North York, ON M3C 2E8   **PRINTED IN U.S.A**

Cat Was Conscious Of His Warmth And His Size.

And of her longing for him. She shivered, but not really with cold. "Come in. Please."

"I will. But first, I..." Dillon seemed not to know how to go on.

She searched his face. "What?"

"I have some...things in the back. Groceries and things. They'll freeze if I—"

"I understand. Let me get my jacket and I'll help you bring them in." She started to turn.

He grabbed her arm. "No. Wait."

She looked up at him, bewildered. "Dillon—what is it?"

"Oh, hell," he said grimly. "Just wait here." For a moment he disappeared, as Cat stood by the door.

At last, he reappeared. Cat blinked when she saw him.

He was carrying a fluffy pink blanket. Cat realized it was a baby when she heard it cry.

Dear Reader,

Here at Desire, hot summer months mean even *hotter* reading, beginning with Joan Johnston's *The Disobedient Bride,* the next addition to her fabulous Children of Hawk's Way series—*and* July's *Man of the Month.*

Next up is *Falcon's Lair,* a sizzling love story by Sara Orwig, an author many of you already know—although she's new to Desire. And if you like family stories, don't miss Christine Rimmer's unforgettable *Cat's Cradle* or Caroline Cross's delightful *Operation Mommy.*

A book from award winner Helen R. Myers is always a treat, so I'm glad we have *The Rebel and the Hero* this month. And Diana Mars's many fans will be thrilled with *Mixed-up Matrimony.* If you like humor, you'll like this engaging—and *very* sensuous—love story.

Next month, there is much more to look forward to, including *The Wilde Bunch,* a *Man of the Month* by Barbara Boswell, and *Heart of the Hunter,* the first book in a new series by BJ James.

As always, your opinions are important to me. So continue to let me know what you like about Silhouette Desire!

Sincerely,

Lucia Macro
Senior Editor

Please address questions and book requests to:
Silhouette Reader Service
U.S.: 3010 Walden Ave., P.O. Box 1325, Buffalo, NY 14269
Canadian: P.O. Box 609, Fort Erie, Ont. L2A 5X3

CHRISTINE RIMMER
CAT'S CRADLE

SILHOUETTE *Desire*®
Published by Silhouette Books
America's Publisher of Contemporary Romance

If you purchased this book without a cover you should be aware that this book is stolen property. It was reported as "unsold and destroyed" to the publisher, and neither the author nor the publisher has received any payment for this "stripped book."

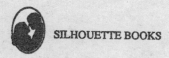

SILHOUETTE BOOKS

ISBN 0-373-05940-X

CAT'S CRADLE

Copyright © 1995 by Christine Rimmer

All rights reserved. Except for use in any review, the reproduction or utilization of this work in whole or in part in any form by any electronic, mechanical or other means, now known or hereafter invented, including xerography, photocopying and recording, or in any information storage or retrieval system, is forbidden without the written permission of the editorial office, Silhouette Books, 300 East 42nd Street, New York, NY 10017 U.S.A.

All characters in this book have no existence outside the imagination of the author and have no relation whatsoever to anyone bearing the same name or names. They are not even distantly inspired by any individual known or unknown to the author, and all incidents are pure invention.

This edition published by arrangement with Harlequin Enterprises B.V.

® and TM are trademarks of Harlequin Enterprises B.V., used under license. Trademarks indicated with ® are registered in the United States Patent and Trademark Office, the Canadian Trade Marks Office and in other countries.

Printed in U.S.A.

Books by Christine Rimmer

CHRISTINE RIMMER

is a third-generation Californian who came to her profession the long way around. Before settling down to write about the magic of romance, she'd been an actress, a sales clerk, a janitor, a model, a phone sales representative, a teacher, a waitress, a playwright and an office manager. Now that she's finally found work that suits her perfectly, she insists she never had a problem keeping a job—she was merely gaining "life experience" for her future as a novelist. Those who know her best withhold comment when she makes such claims; they are grateful that she's at last found steady work. Christine is grateful, too—not only for the joy she finds in writing, but for what waits when the day's work is through: a man she loves who loves her right back and the privilege of watching their children grow and change day to day.

Prologue

Overhead, the desert night exploded with fireworks: trailing comets, rockets, bursting stars. It was the Fourth of July in Las Vegas, and Dillon McKenna was about to jump a motorcycle over the man-made volcano that erupted every fifteen minutes in front of the Mirage casino.

The crowd seemed to stretch out forever along the Strip. Dillon cruised down the middle of the street, working the crowd like the pro he was. He popped a few wheelies. He rose with a quick, agile leap and stood on the seat. For a moment, as he balanced like a wirewalker, he let go of the handlebars and carefully straightened to his full height. He bowed.

The crowd went nuts. They waved their miniature American flags and threw their red, white and blue hats in the air.

Under his breath, as he bent for the handlebars again, Dillon muttered a low curse. It was hotter than hell's basement in the heavy crash helmet and the star-spangled jumpsuit that L.W. had ordered made especially for this jump. Sweat ran in Dillon's eyes, burning. He blinked to clear it away.

He thought, *This is the last jump for me. After this, I'm done.*

The thought soothed him somehow. Made him care a little more about doing it right for the people this last time around.

The people had been good to him, over the years. They deserved a good show. They didn't know that he was quitting. Nobody knew yet.

Dillon slid his feet off the sides of the seat and dropped. His boots landed neatly back on the pegs. He waved. The people screamed and stomped and waved frantically in return.

He'd reached Flamingo Road. Time to turn it around and head for the ramp. A voice from the small speaker inside his helmet told him he had two minutes before the volcano went off. He raced the engine, letting off the clutch just enough to make the tires scream and skid as he turned the bike. Then he gunned it again. The bike, which he'd modified himself for this jump, sounded good to him. It sounded just fine.

All up and down the Strip the chant had begun.

"Dil-lon. Dil-lon. Dil-lon. Dil-lon..." A thousand voices speaking as one. To Dillon the sound was barely more than a whisper beneath the roar of the bike.

"One minute," the voice from the speaker inside his helmet warned. Then the countdown began. "Fifty-nine seconds, fifty-eight..."

Dillon gunned the engine again. He let out the clutch. The faraway chant of the crowd faded to nothing as he shot forward, picking up speed, headed for the takeoff ramp that rose over the lagoon at the foot of the volcano. He hit the base of the ramp and zoomed for the jump. Ahead and beneath him, the eruption began. A sharp, high burst of fire.

He took off from the ramp and soared out into the half block of nothingness going seventy-five miles per hour, with fire belching skyward below him. He rocketed higher, higher, leaving the people and the fire behind. He was standing on the foot pegs, gripping the handlebars, leaning forward, his eyes on the landing ramp, his mind on trajectories, on the arc of himself and the machine. And then he was over the top, into his descent, heading right on course for the landing.

He felt the heavy thud all through him as his rear wheel came down on the lip of the ramp. For a fraction of a second, he thought he was home free.

But then everything went wrong.

Too fast! I've hit the ramp too damn fast!

The thought came blasting into his mind as the bike came alive beneath him, fighting him. The handlebars ripped themselves free of his hands.

Nothing held him. He left the bike and catapulted into the air. He fell, somersaulting, noting in a distant way that beneath him, fire had rimmed the volcano and was beginning to bleed down the sides to set the lagoon aflame.

He came down hard on the ramp in front of the runaway bike. Man and bike became tangled. Over and over they tumbled toward the hard pavement below.

The last thing he heard before he blacked out was his dead father's taunting voice echoing in his head.

*It's your last jump, all right, you worthless piece of
trash. 'Cause you're a dead man...*

He was back in his hometown of Red Dog City, California, standing on the Beaudines' front porch. It was a
fall evening. He could smell burning leaves. There was a
chill in the air. He was seventeen years old. And mean Cat
Beaudine was telling him off.

"All I asked was that you get my sister in by nine, Dillon McKenna. One little request. And you couldn't manage it."

Adora, Cat's sister and his high school sweetheart, was
holding on to his arm. He wanted to impress Adora. And
he wanted to show Cat Beaudine that he was at least as
tough as she was.

He opened his mouth to tell Cat Beaudine just what he
thought of her.

No words came out.

The porch faded away. Someone said something about
vital signs. Faces in surgical masks looked down at him.
The eyes above the masks showed concern. From behind
the masks came soothing words. About how he was all
right. He was going to be all right.

And then he was back on the Beaudine porch again and
Cat Beaudine was raising her daddy's double-barreled
shotgun and aiming it right at his heart.

That was when he knew this wasn't real. In real life, Cat
Beaudine had never actually pointed that gun at him;
she'd only threatened that she might.

In the dream—or the hallucination or whatever it was—
he could talk now. He asked Cat Beaudine, "Why do you
care what your sister does? Why do you care if she gets
home at night?"

Cat answered, "Somebody's got to care. Somebody's got to keep this family together. It's not a job I volunteered for, Dillon McKenna, but it's the job I got stuck with. It's a school night. You said you'd get her in by nine."

He was still staring down those double barrels. He watched in disbelief as Cat disengaged the safety and wrapped two fingers around the twin triggers.

He threw his hands up, shouting, "Hey, you can't shoot me just for keeping Adora out an hour late!"

But Cat pulled the trigger anyway.

And pain erupted through him, white and hot. Teeth of fire dug his flesh away.

And somebody said, "Where's the anesthesiologist? We're only waiting for the anesthesiologist...."

Much later, he swam toward consciousness. The pain was different now. It was still there, still eating him alive, but they must have given him something powerful to ease it. Now the pain seemed to be consuming him from a distance. He knew it was bad, the worst he'd ever experienced. But it was kept at bay somewhere, waiting for the medication to wear off just a little so it could leap on him and devour him whole.

He turned his head and cautiously opened his eyes. An IV drip stood by the metal side rail of the bed. It was hooked up to his arm. There was some machine close by that made little bleeping sounds, like bubbles singing underwater. The air smelled of disinfectant overlaid with the scent of flowers. The flowers were everywhere, intended, no doubt, to cheer up the invalid: him.

And there were voices, from across the room.

They whispered to each other.

"My God, L.W. I just can't."

"You can. You will. McKenna needs you now."

"They say he may never *walk* again. He may be in a wheelchair for the rest of his life. It's too awful, too ugly, I just can't—"

"For God's sake, Natalie. Get a grip on yourself. He's waking up."

He looked toward the sound of the voices. Two familiar faces swam into focus. Natalie, the woman he had meant to marry. And L.W., the man who'd made his name a household word. Both of them were looking right back at him, their mouths stretched into big, brave smiles.

He felt sorry for them, in a removed sort of way. He wasn't going to be much use to either of them now. Just as neither of them was going to be much use to him. Because he didn't kid himself. He'd been broken up enough in his time to have a vague idea of what he was in for. He may have survived his final jump after all. But hell was still waiting for him—a living hell.

A sharp longing pierced him, worse, in a way, than the pain that waited to eat him alive.

It was a longing for home. And for the kind of woman who could take the tough times; a woman strong enough to stand by his side while he endured the months of torment and superhuman effort that were coming up next.

One

Eighteen months later....

Cat Beaudine stood in the doorway of her sister's bedroom. She took in the room at a glance. On the dresser, the small color television soundlessly played the 11:00 p.m. news. There were balled-up tissues everywhere, looking like sad, crumpled paper flowers, used and discarded in drifts and trails across the pink satin sheets of the bed. In the center of the crumpled satin, surrounded by all those used tissues, Cat's sister, Adora, lay sprawled facedown sobbing forlornly.

Adora's most recent boyfriend, Farley Underwood, had left her. And, as always, Adora had called Cat.

Slowly, as if it pained her to lift her head, Adora looked up. She let out a strangled cry. Then she reared back on her knees, her tousled brown hair curling enchantingly around her pretty, flushed face, her cream silk negligee slipping off one shoulder. "Oh, Cat!"

Cautiously Cat approached the bed.

Adora dabbed at her streaming eyes with a wadded-up tissue. "Oh, Cat. Thanks for coming. For always being there over all the years. For being the best big sister in the world. I don't know what I'd do...without you." With a desolate moan, Adora held out her arms.

Cat sank to the edge of the bed and allowed herself to be enveloped in her sister's misery and the heady scent of Adora's perfume.

Adora moaned against Cat's heavy winter jacket. "I'm sorry. To be such a pain. But I had to have someone. Some family. You understand, don't you?"

Cat made a small, sympathetic sound; all that was required at the moment.

Adora sobbed on. "Why me? What is it about me? Why does every man I ever meet end up dumping me? All I ever wanted was what my two baby sisters have. A good man. A family. Someone to take care of me and someone *I* can take care of in return. Is it too much to ask? Is it unreasonable to hope for?" Adora gave another quivering whimper. "Is it?"

"No, of course it's not."

"Of course it's not!" Adora picked up Cat's words and gave them back in a wail. "But it never happens. I'm thirty-four years old. How long do I have to wait? And I'm not like *you,* Cat, perfectly happy wandering around the woods in work boots and baggy jeans with no man in sight, wanting to live out in the middle of nowhere alone in some ancient, run-down shack. I'm just a woman. An ordinary woman. I want a *home,* with nice window treatments and a baby on the way."

Adora surrendered to a fresh fit of weeping. Cat held her and made the required soothing sounds. Eventually Adora calmed a little. Then Cat put her arm around Adora and said the things she always said whenever Adora lost a boyfriend.

"You're too good for him.... You're better off without him.... Someone terrific will come along soon...."

Adora listened, tucked up in the hollow of Cat's shoulder, and made tiny, woebegone noises of agreement.

"Oh, Cat. Do you really think the right man could still come along?"

"Of course I do. I promise you. It's only a matter of..."

But Cat didn't get any farther, because Adora wasn't listening. Adora was gaping at the television instead.

"Omigod!" Cat's sister exclaimed in an ecstatic whisper.

Cat looked at the television. One of those late-night talk shows had come on. A host Cat didn't recognize was interviewing some dark-haired hunk in designer jeans and fancy alligator boots. "What? What is it?"

Adora clutched a wadded-up tissue to her breast and pointed at the television. "It's Dillon. Dillon McKenna. Turn it up. Cat, turn it up!" When Cat didn't move, Adora frantically fumbled around under the mountain of pillows at the head of the bed and came up with a remote control, which she pointed at the television. The sound came on.

"So, Dillon." The host held up a book with a photograph of a gruesomely wrecked motorcycle on the dust jacket. Beneath the crumpled motorcycle, the word *Daredevil* was printed in letters that seemed to be on fire. "Tell us about this book you've written."

Cat made a low noise of disbelief. "Oh, please. Dillon McKenna never wrote a book. I don't buy that for a minute."

"Shh!" Adora hissed and craned forward toward the small screen. "Oh, God. He looks *wonderful....* You can't even see how bad he was hurt in that awful crack-up in Las Vegas. He looks just like before."

On the screen, the dark-haired hunk began to talk. "Well now, if you look down in the corner there, you'll see that *I* didn't write it." He nudged the slender, serious-looking man sitting next to him. "Oliver here did that. He's the writer."

Oliver picked up his cue. "But the story is authentic. Just as Dillon told it to me. From his early days in rodeo, through his years as a movie stuntman, right up to the challenges he set himself. Nothing's missing. There's every jump he ever accomplished, including that baker's dozen Peterbilt semitrucks at the Anaheim Speedway. And, of course, the story finds its climax in Dillon's spectacular, near-death experience in Las Vegas just a year and a half ago."

Cat watched her sister watching Dillon McKenna. Adora's face wore a dreamy, faraway look. Farley Underwood might never have existed.

"Dillon really did turn out to be a fantastic-looking man, didn't he, Cat?" Adora asked.

Cat didn't even bother to look at the man on the screen. One answer was expected of her. She gave it. "Sure."

On the television, the host asked, "So what's up next for Dillon McKenna?"

"You know, I gotta say I'm not sure."

"No kidding?"

"Yeah. Things are going to be different for me, that's all I know for certain. I think what I need right now is a real change of scene, a little time away from it all, to decide where I'm going from here.''

Cat only half listened to the rest. She busied herself gathering up some of the drifts of discarded tissues and tossing them into the wastebasket in the corner, waiting for the next commercial break.

At last, her sister raised the remote control and punched the Mute button again. Then Adora sighed. "Oh, Cat. He made good, didn't he? Dillon really made good.''

There was no arguing with that. Cat smiled. "He certainly did.''

"Did you hear what he said, about not knowing what he was going to do next? About how he's thinking he needs a little time away from it all?''

"Yeah, I heard it.''

Adora's emerald eyes were shining. "Do you imagine he might come back home?''

Cat imagined no such thing. The way she saw it, there was absolutely no reason on earth why an international celebrity like Dillon McKenna would want to return to the tiny mountain town of Red Dog City.

"Well?'' Adora prompted.

"Well, what?''

"You heard me. Don't you think that he might come home?''

"No, I don't.''

Adora frowned. Cat's answer had not been the one she'd hoped for. But then she brightened again. "If he did, you'd be the first to know, wouldn't you? After all, you take care of his house.''

Cat picked up a few more tissues and aimed them at the wastebasket, achieving a swift series of slam dunks. Then she pointed out patiently, "Adora, he hasn't stayed there even once since I've been caretaker of that place. He rents it out through the real estate agency that hired me to take care of it. It's just income property to him.''

"Well, I know. But still. It's a nice house. If he wanted to get some time to himself, to think about life and things, that house would be just the place to go.''

Cat reached for her sister's hands and clasped them firmly in her own. "Look.'' She put her forehead against Adora's. "Will you forget Dillon McKenna? Think about yourself. Are you feeling better now?''

Adora pulled her hands free and fiddled with her shredded tissue. "I guess you want to go home and go back to bed, huh?''

"I'd be lying if I said no. But I'll stay if you—''

"No. Really. Seeing Dillon again kind of cheered me up. I suppose I'll be all right now. At least all right enough to make it through the night.''

"Good.'' Cat bent forward to brush her lips against Adora's cheek.

Adora forced a brave smile. "Thanks again. I mean it.''

Cat stood. "I'm at home if you need me.''

"I know.''

TWO

Dillon McKenna climbed down from his Land Cruiser, ignoring the dull throb in his artificial hip joints as he did it. The snow on the ground made a crisp, crunching sound under his boots.

The house looked good, he thought. From this side, it was all natural colored wood and soaring angles. The other side, which faced the deck and a deep ravine, was floor-to-ceiling windows so that even on the darkest days, the place was full of light.

Dillon took in a big breath, savoring the cold, mountain freshness of the air. From a nearby fir tree, a chickadee trilled at him. And from somewhere not far away came the *thwack*ing sound of an ax splitting wood. Beneath a spruce tree at the side of the driveway a blue pickup was parked: the caretaker's, Dillon imagined. Dillon shut the door of the Land Cruiser, flipped up the collar of his sheepskin jacket and followed the sound of the ax.

He didn't have to go far. Around the other side of the house, on the little ledge of level ground that extended below the deck before the land dropped off into the ravine below, he found the caretaker. The man's back was turned to Dillon and for a moment, Dillon stood and watched him.

Rhythmically and efficiently, the man sunk his ax into a log, lifted the log high and brought it down on the chopping block. Bemused, Dillon admired the grace of movement, the economy of each stroke.

He smiled to himself. Nineteen months ago, he wouldn't have looked twice. But there was something about having half the bones in your body broken, about being put back together with plastic and metal and a good surgeon's gall, that made a man appreciate the simple things—like watching a skinny caretaker whack up the firewood.

Just then, the caretaker seemed to sense that he was being observed. He brought the ax down so it bit into the block. Then, leaving the ax stuck there, he straightened and turned.

Dillon noticed right away that the fellow had delicate features and smooth golden skin. But it took him a few seconds to register that the man also had breasts—high, round breasts, which very nicely filled out the front of his—er, *her*—worn red flannel shirt.

As Dillon gaped, the man who had turned out to be a woman removed the work gloves she was wearing and shoved a hand through her shock of short, raggedly cropped straw-colored hair. Then she squared her slim shoulders and strode purposefully toward him.

As she drew closer, he noted that her eyes were the shimmering gray-blue of a scrub jay's wings. Recognition dawned in those eyes at precisely the moment *he* realized who *she* was: Adora's overprotective big sister, Cat Beaudine.

Home at last.

The thought rose from the depths of him and bloomed on the surface of his mind. It occurred to him that he'd dreamed of her, though he couldn't remember when or what the dream had been about.

"Dillon? Dillon McKenna?" Her disbelief was clear in her voice.

He felt a wide smile break across his face. "The very same. Hello, Cat."

Now *she* was the one gaping. Dillon could understand that. Aside from a possible occasional glimpse of him on the news or in a magazine, she hadn't seen him in about sixteen years. She very well might have been at his father's funeral seven years ago, but he didn't remember seeing her then. In any case, it had been a long time. It would naturally take her a minute or two to get used to the changes time makes. Seeing *her* again had sure given *him* a jolt.

Dillon stuck out his hand. They shook. Her palm was rough, callused from hard work. Her bones, though, were fine and long. He let his gaze wander, noting the dew of moisture on her upper lip and the charming way her pale hair curled, damp and clinging, at her temples. Her body heat came off of her in waves after her efforts with the ax. Her scent, on the cold winter air, was both sweet and faintly musky.

Within his own, her hand jerked a little. He realized he'd held on longer than was probably appropriate. Reluctantly he let her go.

She forged ahead with the pleasantries. "How are you?"

"All grown-up now."

A small vertical line appeared between her brows. "Yes. Yes, I see that." She sounded preoccupied suddenly—and not pleased at all that he wasn't a kid anymore.

Dillon felt jubilant. He was thoroughly enjoying himself. She was exactly the way he'd remembered her. Except for one thing: back then, he hadn't thought her intriguing in the least.

"Ahem. Well." Now she was making a big deal of pulling her gloves back on—to let him know she was returning to the chopping block, he imagined. "This *is* a surprise. When the agency called to tell me to open up the house, I figured—"

"That the new occupant was just another one in the endless chain of short-term tenants?"

She nodded. "But then, I suppose I should have expected it might be you, now I think about it. We heard you were looking for a little time away from it all."

"Where'd you hear that?"

She looked away for a moment, as if she hesitated to tell him. Then she shrugged. "You said it. On some late-night TV show a few weeks ago."

He couldn't resist a little jab. "I'm surprised you were watching. You never were a big fan of mine."

She looked right into his eyes then. "Hey. Out here in the wilderness, we like to keep informed about the ones who made it big. And you picked the right place if you want to be alone. Six miles outside of Red Dog City in the dead of winter is about as alone as anybody could want to get."

He chuckled. "It's less than forty miles to Reno, in case I get too lonely."

"Those can be very rough miles when the heavy snows come."

"I know that. I *was* raised in these parts." He dared to tease her. "Are you trying to get rid of me already, Cat?"

She didn't smile. "No, of course not."

"Good. Because I'm here to stay—for a while, at least."

"Well, that's your business."

"You've got it right there."

They stared at each other. Then she coughed. "Listen, I'm sure you want to get comfortable. You'll find the house was cleaned from top to bottom."

"By you?"

She shook her head. "I don't clean houses. The agency hires a service for that." She went on briskly, "The water's on and I turned on the heat a couple of hours ago, so it should be pretty warm by now. I was just trying to get in a little more wood, in case you'd also like a fire. I don't know who took care of delivering your wood for you, but most of the logs are too big for your stove."

Dillon experienced the most ridiculous urge then. He wanted to march over to where her ax was embedded in the block and hack up a few logs himself, just so she'd know he was as much of a man as she was. The urge totally astonished him. Lately Dillon thought of himself as grown beyond minor displays of masculine ego.

And besides, he'd probably only end up doing damage to himself if he started showing off with an ax right now. He was still learning to control all the new pins and balls he had where a lot of his joints used to be.

"So anyway," she was saying, "I'll just get back to work. I'll finish up here, then carry a load inside and lay the fire for you."

He had a better idea. "Listen, forget splitting any more wood for now."

"But I—"

"Just bring a load into the house and get the fire started. I'd appreciate that."

"Okay, I—"

"And then we'll have a beer."

It took her a moment to absorb that suggestion. Then the protests began. "No, I—"

"Come on. For old times' sake."

Her glance collided with his for a moment, then shifted away. "No, really, I—"

"Yes."

She looked at him again, stared straight into his eyes and tried to shake her head. She didn't succeed. "All right." The minute the words were out, her face flushed a captivating shade of pink beneath her tan.

"Good." He strode toward her and brushed past, leading the way before she could change her mind. "The beer's in my truck. I'll get it and join you inside."

From behind him she made a strangled little sound that was probably the beginning of a protest. He didn't wait to hear the end of it, but trudged away from her as quickly as his rebuilt hips and reconstructed left knee would carry him.

By the time he'd put the Land Cruiser in the garage and let himself into the kitchen, she was standing on the other side of the glass door that opened onto the deck, her arms loaded with firewood. She spotted him through the glass and telegraphed a questioning look. He set down the bag of groceries and the six-pack of long necks he'd brought in with him and hurried across the huge main living area to let her in.

Once inside, she tossed the wood into the box by the wood stove, then pulled off her gloves and stuck them in a back pocket. Dillon went to get two beers from the six-pack on the counter as she knelt to lay and light the kindling. He took a few minutes to empty the bag of groceries and when he returned, she was feeding in a couple of midsize logs. That done, she rose.

He handed her a beer. They both drank. Through the window of the stove, the fire licked at the wood, a cheerful sight.

Dillon gestured in the general direction of a couch and two chairs, which were grouped nearby. "Have a seat."

Cat shook her head and looked down at her old shirt and khaki work pants. "That couch is beige. And I've been under the house checking the pipes."

He started to tell her he couldn't care less about the damn couch. But then he decided that the state of her clothing was only an excuse. She didn't want to sit down. She didn't want to get too comfortable.

He let it pass and stared out the wall of windows. Beyond the deck the world seemed to drop away into a sea of snow-laden evergreen. In the distance, the mountains overlapped each other, disappearing into a gray veil of afternoon mist.

"I can hardly believe I'm here," he mused aloud after a moment. He glanced around the big room and then out the windows at the spectacular view once again. "God. It's beautiful."

"Yes."

He lifted the beer and drank, then found himself telling her, "I bought this house seven years ago."

She made a sound of polite interest, but said nothing.

"It was after my father died. I saw an ad for the place while I was here, so I drove out to see it. I fell in love with it and took it. I think it made me feel that I'd arrived, the fact that I could buy a vacation house just because the mood struck me.''

She spoke then, her tone matter-of-fact. ''You've done well for yourself, Dillon. You have a right to be proud.''

He studied her, thinking about changes. Pondering the effects of time. Deciding that the way a man saw the world sometimes changed more than the world itself. Like the woman before him.

Sixteen years ago, he hadn't seen the deep inner calm she possessed. Or the world of strength and dignity in her eyes. Hell. Back then, he hadn't given a damn for strength and dignity in a woman. He'd thought her tough and mean—and she had been. He was sure she still was when circumstances demanded.

''We heard you had a bad accident a while ago,'' she said.

''Yeah. I jumped a man-made volcano at the Mirage in Las Vegas. The jump was a success. Unfortunately my landing left a lot to be desired.''

Now her eyes were kind. ''I'm sorry.''

''Hey. Breaks of the game.''

''Well, at least you look as if you're recovering well enough.''

''More or less. Everything works, just slower and stiffer.'' He raised his beer and drank. ''So tell me about home.''

''What about it?''

''Well, the Beaudine family, for starters, I suppose. You can tell me how your mom is and how all your sisters turned out.''

She fiddled with the label on her beer bottle, as if she suspected he'd just thrown her a trick question. ''My mother's remarried.''

"No kidding?"

"Yep. Just a few years ago, to a retired housepainter. She met him playing bingo over at the community hall. You could say he sort of swept her off her feet, I guess. They tied the knot a few months after they met and they live in Tucson now."

"What about the little ones?"

"Phoebe and Deirdre?"

"Yeah."

"They're not so little anymore. Both married, as a matter of fact. Deirdre lives in Loyalton. And Phoebe's in Portola."

"Not too far away, then?"

"Right." She took another sip of beer.

"And how about you? Are you married?"

"Me?" She looked surprised that he'd ask such a question. "No, not me."

It was the answer he'd expected, but still, he'd wanted to be sure. He was tempted to probe a little deeper on the subject, to ask her why not? just to see how she'd answer. But he decided against that. She was too edgy. Any probing on his part would probably send her flying out the door.

He kept it light and predictable. "How about nieces and nephews? Got any of those yet?"

"Five." She was fiddling with the bottle's label again. "Deirdre has three daughters. And Phoebe has two boys."

"Wow. Now that's hard to picture. Not only married, but with kids. They were just little girls when I left."

She sipped from her beer again, looked away and then back.

He went on with the next question. "And what about Adora?"

He saw that he'd blown it as soon as the name was out of his mouth. Cat's hand tightened around the beer bottle. A moment before she'd been edgy, but now she was ready to get the hell out. He knew exactly what was going through her mind: What in the world was she doing here, sharing a beer with her sister's old flame?

She forced a tight smile and proceeded to tell him all about Adora. "Adora is just fine. Still single. She has her own beauty shop, right in town on Bridge Street. It's called the Shear Elegance Salon of Beauty. She lives in an apartment above the shop."

He cursed his careless mouth, yet saw no choice but to blunder along in the same vein. "So she's doing well, then?"

"Yes, very well." Cat set her nearly empty beer on a side table. "Listen, it really is getting late and I have to get going." She turned for the door.

All Dillon could think of was that she was getting away from him. He reached out and grabbed her arm. "Wait."

She froze, then whipped her head around to gape at him. Her stunned expression told it all: men rarely dared to touch her. And now that a man *was* touching her, she didn't know what to make of it.

She was what—? A year older than he was, if Dillon remembered right. Thirty-five, maybe thirty-six. And right now, looking in her face, he could swear that in all those years, she'd never once moved in ecstasy beneath the hands of a man.

"What?" she asked in an astonished whisper.

Dillon said nothing. He really had nothing to say, except *Don't go,* which he knew wouldn't keep her there. The silence expanded, seeming to fill the large room.

"What do you want?" Her voice still sounded amazed, but there was a little more force in it than a moment ago.

Again, he didn't answer.

Under the heavy fabric of her shirt, her skin was warm and supple, the muscles beneath like flexible steel. She *was* strong. "Let me go." This time it was a command.

Dillon's hand dropped away. There was no further point in holding on, anyway. The moment he'd stolen through the sheer audacity of daring to touch her had passed.

Like a person stirring from a waking dream, Cat blinked and shook her head. He wondered what she'd do next, if she would get mad because he'd grabbed her arm.

He didn't think she would. Not if he handled it right. Not if he gave her an out she could live with—like pretending that nothing at all had occurred. Which it hadn't. Not really. Not yet.

"Listen, thanks for warming things up."

She studied him narrowly for a moment, then shrugged. "No problem."

Her eyes were cool and level. He thought of the winter world beyond the window. To the untrained eye, it might seem a frozen expanse of white. But warm-blooded things moved there, if you knew where to look.

"Is there anything else I can take care of, before I go?"

A provocative remark occurred to him; he chose not to utter it. "No. Everything looks fine."

"Well, then..."

"Thanks again."

She gave a brief, tight nod. Then she turned and left him alone.

Dillon stood before the wall of windows for a long while after Cat was gone. He was feeling good. The best he'd felt in a long, long time.

After the wreck and the disappointments, after the long months of pain and sweat and fear as he forced his legs, through endless hours of physical therapy, to learn to carry him again, it was good to stand by a window in a house he loved and look out over the mountains in winter. It was good to be here. To be home.

And it was also good that Cat Beaudine was so damned competent. Because he'd already decided he was going to need a lot of help from the caretaker to get himself settled in.

Three

"**Well?** Have you seen him?"

Startled, Cat whirled around. Adora stood in the middle of Cat's living room, smiling.

"Feel free to just walk right in," Cat muttered.

Adora looked minimally regretful. "The kitchen door was open."

"Right."

"So. Did you see him?"

"Who?"

"Oh, stop it, Cat. You know very well who."

"Dillon McKenna." Cat said the name with resignation.

"Yes. Dillon." Adora gave a voluptuous little sigh. "Everybody's talking. He stopped in at the grocery store on his way through town. Lizzie Spooner bagged his groceries. And I know darn well that agency you work for must have called you to tell you to open up the house. That's where you've been, isn't it?''

"Yes, I was there for a while," Cat conceded, then hastened to add, "And I also had the house out on Turner Road to see to. And the place on Jackson Pike."

Adora looked reproachful. "I called you three times. Why didn't you call back?"

Cat cast a rueful glance at the answering machine, which sat on her desk beneath the stairs. The message light was blinking. "I just got in myself." She bent to finish the task of adding more logs to the banked fire, which had burned down to coals in her absence. When the logs were in, she shut the door on the side of the stove. "Want coffee?"

"Tea would be nice."

"Tea it is." Cat headed for the kitchen, where she got down two mugs and the can in which she kept the tea bags. Adora wandered into the room behind her. "How do you do it? It totally mystifies me."

"How do I do what?" Cat went to the kitchen stove, which was half electric and half wood burning. On the wood-burning side, a huge kettle simmered. Cat stoked the fire there as she had the one in the front room.

"You know what," Adora said. "How do you live out here in the middle of nowhere without a soul to talk to half the time?"

"I like my privacy." Cat gestured toward the living room, where several tall bookshelves lined every available wall space. "And I read a lot."

"How *in-tel-lect-u-al*." Adora teasingly drew out each syllable, then tipped her head and wondered out loud, "Don't you ever miss all of us together, the way it used to be?"

Cat thought of the house where she'd grown up. It hadn't been a very big house in which to raise four daughters. There had only been one bathroom, which had always been occupied with one female or another putting on makeup or fixing her hair.

"Well, do you miss it?" Adora prompted when Cat didn't answer right away.

"Not as much as I like my privacy." Cat poured water from the kettle over the tea bags.

"*I* miss it." Adora's eyes were as melancholy as her tone. "I'm a *family* sort of person."

"I know." Cat smiled in understanding. It had been hard on Adora when their mother remarried. Charlotte Beaudine Shanahan had always been a man's woman. And from the day she'd met her second husband, her grown daughters had faded to the background of her life. That was just fine with Cat. And Phoebe and Deirdre both had families of their own now. But Adora felt deserted.

"Come on," Cat said gently. "Take off your coat." She indicated the table. "Sit down. Drink your tea."

Adora sat, then slipped out of her coat and draped it behind her on the back of her chair. That accomplished, she grinned at Cat, who'd taken the seat at the end of the table. "Okay. Tell me all about it." She actually rubbed her hands together in delighted anticipation. "You saw him, didn't you?"

Cat restrained a sigh. She didn't even want to think about her unsettling encounter with Dillon McKenna. And she certainly didn't want to *talk* about it.

"Cat. Did you see him?"

Cat wrapped her tea bag around her spoon and squeezed the last few drops from it.

"Oh, come on." Adora let out a little puff of air in disgust. "What is the matter with you? Are you trying to torture me?"

"No, I'm not trying to torture you." Cat set the tea bag on the edge of her saucer and lifted the cup to her lips. "And yes, I saw him." She took a careful sip.

"Oh, I knew it." Adora actually bounced in her chair. "I was right, wasn't I? He needs some time to...reexamine his life. To decide where to go from here."

"He didn't say that in so many words." Cat set the cup back on the saucer. "But I think you're probably right."

Adora preened a little, dipping her tea bag in and out of her cup. "Do I know him or what?"

"Adora..." Cat began, and didn't know how to go on.

"What?"

Cat thought of the reckless, troubled Dillon McKenna who had left town sixteen years ago. And of the self-possessed, disturbingly compelling man she'd met that afternoon.

"What?" Adora demanded. "Talk to me. What?"

Cat spoke carefully. "Well, people change, that's all. You were kids when he left here, both of you, barely eighteen. You've each ... done a lot of living since then."

Adora's soft chin was set. "I know him. He was my first love. A woman knows. What else did you talk about? What happened? Tell me every bit of it."

Cat looked at her sister and wondered if there was any way to terminate this uncomfortable conversation.

"Talk," Adora prompted.

"There really isn't that much to tell," Cat answered, feeling guilty, though there was no reason to. Nothing had happened. Dillon McKenna had offered her a beer. She'd accepted. They'd talked of mundane things.

Adora was blissfully ignorant of Cat's uneasiness. She bounced in her chair some more. "Tell me anyway. Every little dinky word he said."

Seeing no way around it, Cat quickly described her encounter with Dillon, leaving out only those stunning few moments when he'd held on to her arm. When Cat was finished, Adora sat back in her chair and took a sip of her tea. "Well. That sounds good. Very good."

"Adora, it was an exchange of information, nothing more."

"To you, maybe."

"Adora..."

"It was the part where he asked if I was doing well, that was the key, see?"

"No, I don't."

"You told him how I was, and then he asked *again*. He's anticipating. Just like I am. Wondering what it will be like when at last we meet once more." Adora's chair scraped the old linoleum floor as she stood. "I'm going to go to his house and welcome him home. Right now."

"Adora, maybe you ought to just—"

"I'm going." Adora's chin was set in that way it used to get when she was little and their mother told her she couldn't do something she wanted to do.

Cat reminded herself that Adora was a grown woman. If she wanted to go and pay a visit to an old boyfriend, that was Adora's business and nobody else's.

Cat forced a smile. "Suit yourself."

"I will. I most definitely will." Adora scooped up her coat from the back of the chair and shoved her arms into it. Cheeks flushed and eyes aglow, she headed for the door.

The next day was Saturday. Cat's phone rang at nine. Positive it would be Adora with all the details of her reunion with Dillon, Cat let it ring three times before giving in and picking it up.

"Hello, Cat." The deep, warm voice didn't belong to her sister.

An exasperating shiver traveled up the backs of Cat's legs, and then spread out to take over her whole body. She waited for it to fade a little before she spoke.

"Hello, Dillon."

"Listen." He sounded very offhand. "Since yesterday, I've had a little time to go over my situation here."

His *situation?* What did that mean?

"And it looks as if I'm going to need someone to take care of a few things for me."

"What things?" The two words were suspicion personified.

Cat thought she heard a chuckle, but perhaps it was only static on the line. "I need more firewood split, for starters. And I've bought a decent sound system, VCR and big-screen television. I understand you're good with electronic equipment, so I was hoping you would set them up for me. I also ordered a satellite dish that will need to be hooked up. And there's the exercise equipment for the gym downstairs. I was told the delivery crew would assemble it, but you never know. And I have a lot of books—I'd like some bookcases made. I've heard you do carpentry work."

Cat didn't answer. She was thinking that he'd certainly learned a lot about her abilities in the past twenty-four hours.

She was also thinking that he was offering her paying work. And Cat always needed paying work, especially in the winter months, when all the construction jobs were shut down. She was buying her small house and the five acres it sat on. It was a big investment for someone of her limited means.

But Dillon McKenna represented danger—to her peace of mind, if nothing else. Yesterday, he'd grabbed her arm for no reason and not let go until she'd ordered him to. She wanted to believe that was *all* that had happened.

But somehow, she *didn't* believe it.

And then there was Adora, floating out the door yesterday with stars in her eyes....

"Cat?" Dillon prompted, cutting through her thoughts.

"Yes, yes, I'm thinking." Cat cast about for some way to put him off. "Listen, I appreciate the offer, but I'm afraid you'll have to speak with the real estate agency. I can't just—"

"I've already taken care of that."

"Excuse me?"

"I called the agency. They said it was fine with them if you and I wanted to work out our own personal relationship, now that I'll be living here full-time."

Our own personal relationship. Cat didn't think she liked the sound of that at all.

"I'll pay well." He named an hourly figure. It was twice what she would have asked for most of the work he'd described.

Cat thought of her mortgage. She thought of the improvements she wanted to make to her house next summer: new insulation and double-paned windows that would significantly reduce her firewood consumption. Cat's house wasn't like Dillon's. For her, there was no central propane heat to keep the place toasty. She counted on firewood to provide basic heating.

"Do you want to think about it for a day or two, and give me a call back?" He sounded completely relaxed about the whole thing.

And Cat decided she was being ridiculous. Nothing had happened between herself and Dillon McKenna. And nothing *would* happen. He was still recovering from major injuries and needed someone to help him get settled in. And she needed the money.

"No, there's no need for me to think about it," she said. "It sounds fine to me. When do I start?"

There was a millisecond of a pause. She was absolutely positive he was going to say, Right now.

But he didn't. "A lot of the equipment is coming in Monday morning. Could you be here by ten or so?"

She agreed that she could.

An hour later Adora called. Her soft voice vibrated with excitement. "I saw him. He seemed really glad I dropped in. And guess what else?"

"What?"

"He needs help with some projects around the house. And I know how much *you* need any work you can get. So I told him about all the things you can do. He said he was going to call you this morning. Has he?"

"Yes."

"I knew it. Aren't you going to thank me?"

"Thanks," Cat muttered with heavy irony.

As usual, the irony was wasted on Adora. "Anything for my big sis."

Cat hung up the phone knowing exactly what Adora was up to: creating connections. If Cat worked for Dillon, then Adora had another reason to drop in at his house now and then.

It would never have occurred to Adora that throwing Dillon and Cat together could create any problems at all. Adora was ten times prettier than Cat. And besides, Adora knew very well that her big sister simply wasn't interested in men.

* * *

The delivery van with the television, VCR and stereo arrived at Dillon's at nine-fifteen Monday morning. Dillon had them bring it all into the house. He showed them where he wanted the huge TV, and then had them leave the rest of the equipment in the middle of the room. When they were gone, he set about ripping into the boxes, strewing packing material all over the place. He wanted it to look as if he'd really tried to make some progress at getting it all set up on his own, but he just didn't know what he was doing.

He hoped Cat wouldn't think too deeply about this. Because if she did, she just might begin to wonder why a man who could redesign a motorcycle couldn't figure out how to hook up his VCR to his big-screen TV.

When Cat arrived, she found Dillon sitting on the floor in the huge main room. He was surrounded by torn-open boxes and slabs of polystyrene and packing plastic and he was reading what looked like some sort of instruction booklet. Behind him loomed a brand-new television with a gigantic screen.

Dillon looked up. "Thank God you're here."

Cat's stomach felt agitated. Fluttery and strange. She silently ordered the bizarre sensation to go away as she slipped out of her jacket and hung it by the front door.

"What's up?" She schooled her voice to be calm and professional.

Dillon squinted at the booklet he was holding, turning it this way and then that. "Help."

Cat approached warily and peered over his shoulder. The booklet was the instruction manual for hooking up a VCR. In a dry tone, she suggested, "You might try turning that right-side up."

He gave her a mock-threatening scowl. "Don't get smart. Are you here to work or make fun of me?"

Some little devil inside prompted her to deliver a snappy comeback. She quelled the devil. She remained business-like and distant, as she'd promised herself she would be. "What can I do?"

"Sit down." He patted the space right beside him.

She hesitated, thinking it wouldn't be wise to sit too close to him. And then she decided that if she *didn't* sit close to him, he would think she was nervous around him. And she *wasn't* nervous around him. Not in the least.

He held out the booklet. "Come on. Take this. *Do* something about it."

She took the booklet and dropped next to him. Then she did her best to concentrate on the diagram he'd been looking at.

"God," he said.

She shot him a suspicious glance. "What?"

"Oh, nothing. Just wishing."

She knew she shouldn't ask, but she did anyway. "Wishing what?"

He snorted. "That I could get up from here with one-tenth the ease that you got down."

"Do you want to get up? I'll be glad to help you."

He shook his head. "Not yet. I'm working up to it gradually."

This close, she could see that there were little gold flecks in the velvet brown of his eyes. His chin had a cleft in it. Cat seemed to remember that his blade of a nose had once been straighter. He'd probably broken it jumping out of a building for a movie or riding a bucking bronc in a ro-deo.

She couldn't stop herself from asking, "Why did you get down, if you knew it was going to be a problem getting up?"

"Hey, I have to do the tough things, if I ever want them to be anything like easy again."

"*Will* they ever be easy again?"

"It's relative. I'll never run a marathon, if that's what you mean."

They were smiling at each other.

Cat reminded herself once more that she was here to work, not hear all about how Dillon McKenna was dealing with the changes his accident had made in his life. She looked at the booklet again. The page showed the terminals on the back of the VCR. It was a very clear and simple diagram. She glanced up at Dillon, to tell him this little task should be a piece of cake.

But something else entirely popped out of her mouth. "Has it been hard for you?"

He answered frankly. "Yeah. On a lot of levels. But it was time for a change anyway, you know?"

"How so?"

"Well, sometimes, in the past few years, I've found myself wondering exactly what it was I had to prove. Risking my life to jump a pyramid of sixty Buicks on a souped-up Harley started to seem more stupid than heroic to me. And the accident at the Mirage was bad. I've been broken up a lot in my time, but this was the worst. I was on my back or in a wheelchair for six and a half months."

Cat thought of her own good, strong body. She depended on it to perform for her. How would she deal with it if she couldn't walk for six months? Not well, she suspected. Not well at all. "I'll bet you went nuts."

"Yeah. You could say that." He grinned rakishly.

Cat stared at his lips. They were wide and nicely shaped, lips made for rakish grins. There was a faint, jagged scar on his upper lip, like a tiny lightning bolt.

"What's that?" She reached out, almost touched the scar, but stopped herself just in time.

Dillon knew what she meant. He touched the scar himself, lifting his dark brows at her in silent question.

She nodded in confirmation.

"A steer hooked me. Back when I was still riding the rodeos."

"With its *horn*, you mean?"

"You got it. Ripped my lip in half. But that was fifteen years ago. It's faded almost to nothing now." He leaned in closer to her, so she could get a better look.

Cat leaned in, too, though she could see perfectly fine from right where she was. She realized that the gold specks in his eyes seemed to be glittering, like tiny flakes of pyrites in a mountain stream. And she also liked the smell of him. A clean smell, with a hint of something else, a little like cedar, tangy and sharp.

Right then, the door chimes rang.

Cat jerked bolt upright as a hot blush went shooting straight up to the roots of her hair.

"I . . . um . . ."

But Dillon seemed totally unconcerned. "Great. That's probably the equipment for the gym."

She took her cue from him. After all, if he thought nothing had happened, then nothing really had. Had it? She'd only leaned in close to look at that scar on his lip, that was all.

He smiled ruefully. "Either help me up from here—or answer that, will you?"

"Sure. No problem. I'll get it." She leapt to her feet and flew to the door.

It was the gym equipment. Since Dillon had to sign for it and show them where he wanted it, she helped him get up as soon as she let in the two delivery men.

The main living area of the house was upstairs, including the master suite. Downstairs was a central room off of which branched three more large rooms and two baths. One of those rooms had been intended for a gym; its walls were lined with mirrors. The equipment had to go in there.

Once everything was inside, it turned out that the delivery men actually were fully trained in assembly of the equipment. So Cat left Dillon to supervise them and went back to the upper level to tackle all the electronic gadgets that waited there.

By one in the afternoon, the delivery men took their leave and Cat had the chaos upstairs under control. She showed Dillon how to work all his new electronic toys, pointing out that he wouldn't get anything but a few public stations on his fancy big screen until he either hooked up to cable or brought in that satellite dish he'd mentioned.

He said the dish was due this week. "And let's have lunch. I'm starving."

"I have a sandwich in my truck," she said. "But aren't we done for the day?"

He shook his head. "Don't forget the wood. I like a fire, especially in the evenings. And I seem to have used up nearly all of what you split for me Friday."

That was okay with Cat. As the hours added up, so did the money. "I'll go eat and—"

"What do you mean, you'll go eat?"

"I told you. I have a sandwich in my—"

"It's probably peanut butter and jelly, right?"

She felt defensive. "What's wrong with peanut butter and jelly?"

"So it *is* peanut butter and jelly." He looked ridiculously proud of himself to have guessed. "I knew it. And forget it. You're not going to sit out there on your tailgate, eating peanut butter and jelly in the freezing cold."

"This is silly. It's not that cold. And I like peanut butter and jelly."

"Fine. Save it for a snack later. I'm making lunch."

"But I—"

"Forget arguing. I'm the boss. Don't make a big deal out of this, all right?"

She looked at him measuringly for a moment, feeling one-upped somehow. She was suspicious. But why? He hadn't been any more than casually friendly with her all morning. Had he?

Oh, what was the matter with her? There was *nothing* going on here. Wild Dillon McKenna had grown up into a very nice man who was paying her good money for honest work—and who was willing to throw a free lunch into the bargain.

She had to get real here. These misgivings she kept having about his motives were completely in her own mind. She was Cat Beaudine, after all. She knew the things people said about her when they thought she didn't hear.

That she was tough and strong and someone you could count on. And about as feminine as Paul Bunyan. Men were her friends. Men were her equals. But men never looked at her the way she'd seen them look at her sisters—or even her mother, for that matter.

And there was no reason in the world why Dillon McKenna—who could probably have just about any available woman in the Western Hemisphere—would see her any differently than other men saw her.

She smiled at Dillon. "Well, thanks then. Lunch would be nice."

After she had washed her hands in the half bath off the kitchen, she went and sat at the table. Dillon was just pulling a cooked, cut-up turkey out of the refrigerator.

"Where did you get that?"

"At the store."

"All roasted and cut up like that?"

He confessed that he'd done the roasting and cutting up himself. "I like to cook. Especially lately. It's one of the few things I can do for myself that hardly hurts at all." He got out a cutting board and a big, gleaming knife and began slicing meat off the breast section. Cat's stomach rumbled, the meat looked so good. He winked at her. "You should have seen me in my wheelchair, flying around the kitchen. I was impressive."

"I'll bet."

When he had a nice, tall stack of meat sliced, he got out bread, mayonnaise and lettuce and assembled two fat, wonderful-looking sandwiches. With them, he offered pickles and cranberry sauce and tall glasses of milk.

"You were right," she told him, after the first heavenly bite. "This beats the heck out of peanut butter and jelly."

When lunch was over, Cat went outside and split wood for two hours, carefully re-covering the pile of logs when she was done. Then she carried what she'd split into the garage and stacked it against a wall, so that it would be protected from the elements as well as reasonably easy for Dillon to bring in.

By then, it was growing dark. She was ready to go home. She stuck her head in the kitchen door, thinking she'd just give a yell and tell Dillon she was leaving.

But he was nowhere in sight. When she called, she got no answer. She was forced to step inside.

"Dillon!" She moved through the big kitchen, into the main room. It was then that she heard music, coming from downstairs.

She followed the sound and found him in his newly set-up gym. He was wearing a pair of sweatpants and a T-shirt, standing before one of the walls of floor-to-ceiling mirrors, doing bicep curls with a pair of fat dumbbells. On the floor at his feet was a portable tape player/radio—the kind that kids call a boom box. It was blaring out music by Talking Heads.

As soon as he saw Cat, Dillon put down the dumbbells and switched off the boom box. "Gotta get a stereo in here, too." He straightened again and came toward her.

He was sweating. There were dark stains on his shirt—at the neck, chest, belly and beneath his arms. Little beads of moisture slid off his damp hair and tracked down his flushed face and corded neck.

Cat felt overwhelmed suddenly, by all that heated male flesh. And then she wondered again what her problem was lately. Since she'd been old enough to wield a hammer, she'd spent her summer months working construction crews on whatever building projects came her way. She toiled right alongside a bunch of sweaty guys with their shirts off and she never thought twice about it.

"All finished?" Dillon asked.

"What? Oh. Yeah. All done."

"Same time tomorrow?"

"Tomorrow?"

His expression was bland, but the gold flecks in his eyes seemed to be dancing. "Yeah. You know. The day after today."

"You need me tomorrow?"

"You bet."

"For what?"

"A thousand things."

"Like what?"

"The satellite dish might arrive."

"And what else?"

"Let's talk about it then. Ten o'clock. As usual."

She felt provoked, though she couldn't figure out why. "As usual. What does that mean? I've only worked for you for one day."

"Is this an important point?"

"Of course not. I just want things clear, that's all."

"Fine. What isn't clear to you?" A single crystalline drop of sweat dripped down the bridge of his nose. He swiped at it with the back of his hand. She saw the inside of his forearm, shiny with moisture, as hard as a rock and ropy with tendons and veins. "Well?"

She felt dazed. She couldn't think. "I . . . nothing."

He was smiling again. "Good. I do appreciate this."

Now she felt like a fool. "Of course."

"Tomorrow, then? Ten o'clock."

"Yes. Tomorrow. Ten o'clock."

Four

The satellite dish did not arrive the next day, but Dillon's books did.

He put Cat right to work measuring and estimating the cost for new shelves in the living area and also downstairs in the big central room. Next, he decided a trip to Reno was in order that very day, to purchase the lumber. He insisted they both had to go, since she was the one building the shelves and he was the one buying them.

She told him that there was absolutely no reason he had to go with her to get the lumber.

He gave her a grin that actually looked shy. "Yes, there is. I want to choose the wood myself. Please?"

He was really laying on the charm, she thought, and refused to admit that it was working. She looked away—anywhere but into those coaxing brown eyes—and gestured at all the open boxes of books strewn around the room. "I don't get it. What's this new thing you've got about books?"

He made a *tsk*ing sound. "Now, Cat. Was that a nice thing to say?"

She glanced at him again, wondering what he was up to. "What do you mean?"

He was pretending to look wounded. "You're referring to the fact that I almost flunked out of high school my senior year, aren't you? You can't understand how a loser like I was could have grown up to need a whole houseful of bookcases."

"I did not say you were a loser."

"No, but you thought it. And hey, it's okay. I was a messed-up kid. It's not a secret. But now I'm not a kid anymore. And I like to read. When I first started doing gags for the movies, it was books that kept me sane."

"Gags?"

"Yeah, gags. Stunts. Same thing."

Cat asked, "Why did books keep you sane?" though she'd told herself all last night that when she came in to work for him today she would keep the talk strictly focused on the job at hand.

Dillon was only too happy to forget the job at hand. "In the movies, it's always hurry up and wait. You can wait hours, *days,* for the weather to clear. Or for a shot to be set up. I learned to carry a book along with me all the time. Then when it came time to wait, I had something to occupy my mind."

Another question she had no business asking found its way out of her mouth. "Did you ever go any farther in school?"

He bent, a little stiffly as always since his return home, and snared a book from one of the boxes. He looked at the title on the binding, then gently opened it to the first page. "Nah. Never got around to it—not that any reputable college would take me." He glanced up from the book. "What about you? Did you ever get to college?"

"No," she said quickly, wondering why in heaven's name she'd asked him that question about going farther in school.

"Why not? I seem to remember that you were a real brain. There was even a scholarship, wasn't there?"

Cat stuck her hands into her pockets and looked out the window at the trees and the ever-present winter mist. "Yes."

"What school was it? I forget."

She wanted to tell him she didn't wish to discuss this with him, but that would be making a big deal out of it. And if she made a big deal out of it, he would sense that she often regretted missing her chance for a college education. She didn't want him to know of her regret. It was too personal. And she was being careful to avoid anything personal with him.

"Cat, what school was it?" he asked for the second time.

She made herself look at him. "It was Stanford. An engineering scholarship."

"Stanford. That's right. Why didn't you go?"

"I had to turn it down when my father died—which I'm sure you already know."

His smile was utterly guileless. "Yeah, now that you mention it, I do remember that."

Cat's tape measure was on the table next to her. She grabbed it, marched across the room and dropped it into her tool kit.

"But what about later?"

She knelt to close the lid of the tool kit. "What about it?"

"Why didn't you go to college later?"

She absolutely would not let her fading patience with this conversation show in her voice. She flipped the lid of the tool kit closed and firmly snapped the latch in place. "What does it matter?"

"I'm curious, that's all."

"Look, it just never worked out. Phoebe and Deirdre were so young. And my mom, well, she kind of went to pieces there for quite a while. She'd married my dad when she was eighteen, and she just didn't know how to cope without a man around the house."

"So you had to be the *man* of the family?"

Slowly Cat stood. "Is that some kind of a dig?"

"No. It's just a question. A straight question."

"Fine. Then the answer is yes. In a lot of ways, when my father died, I was the one who took his place. I made decisions my mother wasn't up to making. And I looked out for my sisters. And I brought in enough extra money to make ends meet."

Dillon nodded, as if in acknowledgment of a job well done, then he closed the book he was holding. "So what about now?"

"What about it?"

"You could go to college now."

"It's too late now."

"Not necessarily." He bent a little to put the book back in the box.

"Yes, it is." Her voice sounded level, calm and reasonable. She was glad for that, at least. She longed to tell him to mind his own business. But she wouldn't. She had too much pride. He wasn't going to see that he was getting to her. "I like my life just the way it is. I have my freedom. And my privacy."

"You could have freedom and privacy—and still go to college."

That was it. She would hear no more. "Yes, I could. But then, that's up to me, isn't it?" Her voice dripped sarcasm.

He was grinning again; she could easily have thrown one of his precious books at him. "Yeah, it is. It's up to you." And then he looked at the Rolex on his wrist. "Hey, time's wasting. We should get going."

"Where?"

"To Reno. Remember—the shelves?"

They took Cat's pickup, so they could bring the lumber right back with them.

They reached Reno at a little past noon and Dillon promptly decided he was starving. He made Cat drive around for another half hour, until he saw a restaurant that interested him—a steak house that looked casual and comfortable from the outside.

It was the same inside—except for the prices. Cat took one look at them and decided she could get by with a dinner salad.

"Don't look so grim," he instructed over the top of his menu. "I'm the boss and I'm paying."

She started to argue with him. She always paid her own way. But he *was* the boss, after all. And he had been the one to insist they come here. She'd have been perfectly happy sitting in the cab of her pickup munching on a fast-food burrito.

She decided she'd order the salad as planned—but let him pay for it.

However, when the waiter came and she tried to tell him she wanted a salad, Dillon cut her off and ordered a steak for her. Cat waited until they were alone again to tell Dillon that she was perfectly capable of ordering her own food.

"You're right." He looked properly chastised. "Who the hell do I think I am, anyway? I'm sorry. Do you want me to call the waiter back?"

She stared at him across the table, wondering what it was about him that always kept her off-balance. Just when she was going to put him in his place, he'd always back right off. Then she'd feel that she'd made a big deal over nothing at all. "No. No, it's all right."

Dillon smiled and the lines around his eyes crinkled so he looked handsomer than ever. "Great."

Halfway through the meal, two very pretty women dressed in trim business suits approached the table.

One of them, the taller of the two, cleared her throat and ventured, "Um, excuse us. But aren't you Dillon McKenna?"

Dillon crinkled his eyes at them. "The one and only."

The tall one giggled at the shorter one. "I was right. Can you believe it, Elaine?"

Elaine held out a cocktail napkin with the restaurant's name on it. "I know you probably get sick of stuff like this, but would you . . . ?"

"Be happy to, ma'am."

Elaine brandished a pen. "Here you go."

Dillon took the pen and scrawled his name on the napkin, then returned it, flashing another of those killer smiles of his.

The taller woman, who'd been staring at Dillon as if she were a starving woman with her eye on a slab of prime rib, snapped to attention. "Oh! Don't forget me!" She whipped out a cocktail napkin of her own, which Dillon promptly signed.

"Thank you. Really. Thank you," The two women blushed and stammered, backing away.

Cat watched, thinking that she'd never seen two grown adults look more like awestruck girls. She also wondered what it must be like for Dillon, to have people recognize him everywhere he went. Cat knew she wouldn't like a life in the spotlight. She cherished her privacy too much.

When they arrived back at Dillon's house, they found a green van waiting in the driveway. Tamberlaine Housekeeping Service was printed on the side. As soon as Cat pulled the pickup to a stop, Adora emerged from the van and ran up to Cat's side window.

"Where have you two *been?* I almost gave up."

Cat gestured toward the pickup's bed where the wood for the shelves lay beneath a heavy canvas tarp. "To Reno for lumber. Dillon wants shelves for his books." Somehow, she didn't quite mention that they'd also stopped for a very pricey lunch.

Dillon got out on his side and came around the front of the pickup. "Hey, Dory. What's up?"

Adora turned to him, her smile so bright it hurt Cat's eyes to see it. "The other day you said you needed a housekeeper."

"Do I ever. And if I don't find one soon, I'm going to be forced to deal with that vacuum cleaner that someone put in the hall closet. I would have asked Cat, but—"

Adora waved a hand. "Cat's no good for that. She doesn't do houses."

"I know. She told me the first day I came home."

"Well, it doesn't matter. You can stop worrying. I've solved your problem." Adora turned and called to the driver of the van. "Bobby, get over here!"

Bob Tamberlaine emerged from the van—all six foot five of him. Bob was built like a linebacker. Smiling serenely, he lumbered to Adora's side.

Adora introduced the two men and then Dillon invited everyone into the house. Cat tried to demur, saying she should return to her place and get to work with her table saw on the lumber for the shelves. But Dillon insisted she come in, so she found herself following the others inside.

At Dillon's request, Cat laid and lit the fire in the wood stove. Dillon and Bob reached a swift agreement on what Bob's duties and hours would be.

Then Dillon insisted they all have a drink to celebrate the fact that he wouldn't have to learn to use a vacuum cleaner after all.

Cat said that she really had to get going, but then Dillon stuck a beer in her hand. It was already opened, so she decided to go ahead and drink it before she took off.

Dillon led Adora and Bob downstairs to show off his new gym equipment. Cat stayed upstairs, thinking she should go, and at the same time contemplating how pleasant the big house was, even with all the boxes of books underfoot. Music played on the stereo, the fire crackled in the stove and friendly voices drifted up from the lower floor.

When Dillon and the others returned, they all gravitated to the kitchen. They laughed together. The talk was casual, of the weather, sports and favorite movies. As they talked, Dillon began pulling things from the refrigerator. When he had all his ingredients assembled, he swiftly and efficiently sliced meat and cut up vegetables, all of which he then threw into a big pan, along with some peanut oil and a few spices.

Then he instructed, "Cat, the plates are in that cupboard there. Would you put 'em on the table?"

"Sure." Cat turned for the cupboard.

Adora shot to her feet. "It's all right, Cat. I'll take care of this."

Cat dropped back to her stool as Adora bustled over, got down the plates and carried them to the table.

"Don't set a place for me," Cat said. "I really do have to go."

Dillon looked up from the stove. "No, you don't. Dory, set her a place." He turned back to his work.

Adora blinked and looked from Cat to Dillon, a perplexed expression on her face. Then she put on a bright smile. "Of course I'll set a place for Cat." And she did.

Half an hour later, Cat found herself sitting at the table with the others. The meal that Dillon had whipped up so effortlessly was wonderful. And the conversation flowed pleasantly enough. But more than once, Cat intercepted Adora's quick, assessing glances—from Dillon, to Cat, then back to Dillon again. The looks made Cat uncomfortable. At the same time she told herself they meant nothing. Nothing at all.

It was nearing nine o'clock when Cat finally managed to get herself out the door. Adora and Bob were still there, sitting in the living area around the CD player with Dillon, who was insisting that he had a Jerry Jeff Walker album in his collection somewhere.

Over the next two weeks, Cat worked for Dillon nearly every day. Even after the satellite dish was in place and the books snug in their new shelves, he always seemed to have some extra project for Cat to handle, either something he needed built, or something he'd broken that had to be fixed.

One morning, he broke two of the mirrored panels in his gym. When Cat asked what he could possibly have been up to, he claimed that a barbell had gotten away from him. Of course, he and Cat had to drive straight to Reno and get the replacements, after which he insisted that she install them that very day.

Then he decided to make one of the bedrooms downstairs into a study. He'd need more shelving for that. And he wanted Cat to make him a big, sturdy pine desk, as well.

Cat shook her head. "What do you need a study for?"

He gave her a look of great patience. "I don't *need* a study, Cat. I want one."

"But why?"

"Who knows? I might want to write another book."

"You mean you might want to get that poor, exploited Oliver man to write another book *for* you." Cat had read the book, actually, and found it excellent. But for some reason, she was reluctant to tell Dillon as much, to admit that she worked for him all day—and then had spent two of her evenings reading his life story.

Dillon was scowling at her. "Oliver Ames is far from exploited. His agent is a bloodsucker, the best in the business. He made sure Oliver got a fifty-fifty split."

"But if Oliver wrote it, shouldn't he have gotten more than that?"

"Look, Cat. I want a study. I'm going to have a study. Are you going to make me some shelves and a desk?"

"Hey, it's your money. If you want to throw it away—"

"Good. Come downstairs. I'll show you what I had in mind."

On another day, Dillon dropped a potato peeler down his garbage disposal, managing to get it lodged in there so firmly that Cat had a devil of a time getting it out. Then she found that the cutter blades were so badly mangled the thing was useless. A new unit had to be purchased and installed.

Around noon, when Cat was half inside the cabinet beneath the sink, getting ready to put in the new unit and hoping she had all the replacement washers she was going to need, she heard the doorbell ring.

A few minutes later, Dillon was standing over her. "Cat, this is L. W. Creedy."

Cat pulled her head out from under the sink and looked up at a stout, balding fellow wearing an expensive three-piece suit and a pinkie ring with a diamond in it the size of Lake Tahoe.

"L.W. is the best promoter alive today," Dillon explained.

"Nice to meet you." Cat waved a socket wrench at the man, in lieu of a handshake.

L. W. Creedy waved jauntily and wiggled his bushy eyebrows. "Ah. The handywoman. Always good to have one around." As Cat smiled at him, she tried to remember where she'd heard his name before. It came to her: Dillon's biography. L. W. Creedy was the man who had arranged and publicized many of Dillon's biggest jumps.

Dillon gestured at a kitchen chair. "Park it, L.W."

The promotor grunted as he settled his bulk into the chair. Dillon turned for the refrigerator.

Cat sighed loudly. Over the days she'd worked for him, she'd noticed that Dillon had a thing about fixing meals for people. If a person showed up at his house, he felt honor-bound to feed them something. Cat suspected his need to feed others was some kind of a backlash from his childhood, when Cat knew he'd rarely had enough to eat. It was an endearing trait. But *not* when she had the electricity turned off and the drainpipes out of the sink.

"Please. Could you let me finish this? Maybe take your friend *out* to lunch?"

Dillon was leaning on the open refrigerator door, deciding what culinary masterpiece he would whip up today. He shot her a grin. "I'll only make sandwiches, I promise. And I'll stay out of your way."

Cat scowled at him and stuck her head back beneath the sink.

L.W. continued the conversation that must have been started in the other room. "I'm telling you, McKenna, this could be the biggest thing yet."

Cat heard the refrigerator door shut. "But I'm not interested, L.W.," Dillon said rather wearily. Then he moved to the counter that divided the main room from the kitchen.

"Rattlesnake Ravine," L.W. announced. "You ever heard of it?"

Dillon drew in a long breath. "No."

"Over near Mount Shasta. And I've been talking to the Harley-Davidson people. You gotta see what they're working on. It's an incredible piece of machinery, a jet cycle like you never seen."

"Mayonnaise, L.W.?"

"Just the spicy mustard. You oughtta know that by now. Where was I? Oh, yeah. I figure the Fourth of July would be a great date for it. You know, warm enough up there to get the crowds out. And exactly two years from the thing in Vegas. We can make a lot of that. You know, how they thought you would never walk again—and here you are attempting the most death-defying jump of your incredible career. It's gonna be great. I've got the costume all worked out. We're gonna dress you up like a human flag and—"

"L.W. Why am I not getting through here?" Dillon asked. "I said no. It's a two-letter word meaning, thanks but no thanks. For the thousandth time, it's over. I'm done."

That silenced L.W. For a minute or two. Cat heard the plate clink on the table as Dillon set a sandwich in front of him.

L.W. had a mouthful when he started talking again. "You haven't let it go yet, have you? You're still mad about—"

Dillon cut him off. "I'm not mad. I don't hold it against you. Things just worked out that way, that's all. Don't worry about it."

Cat tried not to wonder what "it" was, other than no concern of hers. She had the new unit up under the sink and was working on getting the wires reconnected.

L.W. said, "You mean that. No hard feelings?"

"Absolutely. It was over before you got involved. Forget about it."

"Great." There was a silence. Then L.W. asked, "Got milk?"

Dillon strode to the refrigerator again. Cat, still struggling with connections under the sink, heard the sound of liquid filling a glass.

"Thanks," L.W. said a minute later. There was quiet again, no doubt for L.W. to drink his milk and gobble down the last of his sandwich. Then Cat heard him ask, "But if you're giving up jumping, what the hell are you going to do with the rest of your life, McKenna?"

Dillon carried something over to the trash can and dropped it in. "Hey. Who can say? Maybe I'll get married and raise a dozen kids. Raising kids is a lot of work, you know. If you do it right."

"Married to who?"

Cat realized she was holding her breath in her cramped position under the sink as she waited to hear Dillon's answer.

Dillon chuckled. "What's it to you who I marry?"

"Hey, just curious."

"Right."

"My God." The promoter sounded pained. "What's happened to you? You once told me you'd shrivel up and die if you didn't put your life on the line on a regular basis."

"You ever raised a kid, L.W.?"

L.W. snorted in disgust. "God, no. I hate the little buggers."

"Well, I've heard it's quite a job. A lot tougher than jumping off buildings and driving jets over ravines, some people would say."

"Right, right. But now you listen. When you change your mind—"

"I won't."

Cat realized she was getting a crick in her neck from holding so still. She shook herself and got back to the job at hand.

L.W. argued some more, but Dillon remained firm. He was out of the daredevil business for good.

The next day, a reporter showed up at the door. He'd heard that Dillon was planning a new stunt, and he wanted to get the scoop on it.

"Who told you I was planning a jump?"

"Sorry, I can't reveal my sources."

"Does his name start with L.W. and end with Creedy, by any chance?"

"As I said, I received the information confidentially."

"Well, tell your confidential source to give it up. Dillon says no. He'll always say no. He is through making jumps."

"But, Mr. McKenna, I—"

"Have a nice day." And Dillon gently closed the door on the fellow.

Two days later, on Friday, Dillon had another visitor.

When she heard the door chimes ring, Cat was in the half bath off the kitchen, replacing a worn-out flapper valve inside the toilet tank. She knew that Dillon was down in his gym with the new stereo in there turned up high. He wouldn't hear the chimes. So she gave the toilet one more test flush to see that all was in working order, dried her hands on a paper towel and went to see who it was.

Cat's breath got stuck in her throat when she pulled open the door. A woman stood on the front porch. A beautiful woman with long hair that shimmered like black silk in the weak winter sun.

The woman smiled...a nervous smile. "Hello. I'm Natalie Evans. I'm looking for Dillon McKenna. Is he here?"

Cat smiled back, ignoring the funny tightness in her chest as she wondered who this woman was to Dillon.

Natalie hastened to explain. "I'm a...personal friend. If you could just tell him it's me."

Cat stepped back so Natalie could come in. "Sure." She gestured toward a couch. "Sit down. I'll get him."

Down in the gym, Tina Turner was shouting her head off through Dillon's fancy new speakers. He turned the volume down when he saw Cat and grabbed a towel that was hanging over the end of a weight bench. "What's up?"

"You have a visitor. Natalie Evans?"

Dillon swore softly under his breath as he mopped sweat from his face and wiped the back of his neck with the towel. Then he forced a grim smile. "Okay. Thanks."

At that moment, Cat realized that all she wanted was out of there. "Um, listen. I'm done with that problem in the half bath. I put in a new valve. The tank's filling properly now. So I think I'll just—"

"Run like hell?" The words were harsh. Her expression must have shown her dismay at his anger, because he chuckled humorlessly. "Not funny, huh?"

"Not particularly."

He sighed. "Okay. So you're taking off?"

"Yes."

"Tomorrow, all right? Say around noon?"

"What for? I'm working on the desk at my place and there's no need for me to—"

"Noon." It was a command.

Cat stared at him as conflicting emotions roiled inside her. A strange, beautiful woman showed up at his door, and all of a sudden, Dillon was a rude stranger. Cat wanted to tell him to go take a hike. And she wanted to soothe him, to tell him it—whatever *it* was—would work out all right. Given the way he'd spoken to her, the urge to tell him to take a hike didn't bother her much. But the desire to give comfort did.

"I want you here at noon," he said again in that imperious tone.

"Fine. Noon." She pushed the words out through clenched teeth.

Then she turned and got out of there, choosing the glass doors in the central downstairs room for her escape over the main entrance upstairs where Natalie Evans waited.

When Cat went around the house to the front and climbed into her pickup, she saw a silver Mercedes parked in the driveway. Natalie Evans was not only beautiful, she also had expensive taste in cars.

That night, Cat seriously considered not going back to Dillon's the next day. She was still smarting from the way he'd spoken to her.

Cat tried to tell herself that Dillon's attitude was the only reason she wanted to stay away. But there was more to it, she knew. And that *really* bothered her.

So she refused to dwell on it at all, and returned to Dillon's at noon as she'd agreed.

When she arrived, the silver Mercedes was nowhere in sight. Inside, Dillon was at the stove, stirring what smelled like a pot of clam chowder. He glanced over his shoulder at her when she entered the kitchen.

"Just in time. Have a seat."

She thought of how he'd insisted she be here. And now it appeared there was nothing for her to do. She could be taking care of other things. She could be finishing up that desk he just *had* to have.

She told him, "I came here to work. Not to eat."

His big shoulders sketched a lazy shrug, but she could feel the tension radiating off him. "I'll find some work for you to do later. Let's eat first, though."

She thought about his words. I'll *find* some work for you to do.... If he had to *find* the work, then he certainly didn't need to have her here.

She shouldn't have come. She was sure of that now.

She didn't like this. Not any of it. Not Natalie Evans, who'd appeared out of nowhere and then vanished the same way. Not his insistence that Cat be here at noon for what apparently was only lunch. And not her own feelings, which were as muddled and confused as this weird situation.

"What's going on?"

He ladled the soup into a big tureen. "Sit down. We'll talk as soon as we've had some lunch."

"I don't want lunch."

"Humor me. Eat it anyway."

"No."

He turned from the stove to level an I-mean-business look at her. "Then don't eat. Just sit down."

They stared at each other for an endless moment. It was a battle of wills. Cat lost. She dropped into a chair in front of a bowl and spoon.

Dillon crossed to the table, set the tureen on a trivet next to a basket of rolls, then sat down as well. He filled Cat's bowl and then his own.

Cat kept her hands in her lap. She looked down at the steaming chowder and then up at Dillon, who was paying a great deal of attention to unfolding his napkin and laying it over his knees.

"I know how you are about food, Dillon. But in this case, food is not going to fix anything," she told him as patiently as she could manage, given the circumstances.

As if she hadn't spoken, he picked up his spoon and started to eat.

"Dillon. I'll ask you one more time. What is going on?"

Dillon had his spoon halfway to his mouth. He dropped it. It landed with a splash in his bowl, splattering soup on the black sweater he wore.

He picked up his napkin and carefully wiped the splatters away. "You want to talk *now?*" His voice was very soft.

"Yes."

"Fine." He tucked his napkin beneath the rim of his bowl. "We'll talk *now*— Where shall we start?"

Her heart did a funny flip-flop in her chest. Now that he was willing to talk, she wasn't sure it was such a good idea. "Well, I..."

"How about Natalie? You're going nuts, thinking about Natalie—and who she is and what she means to me. Aren't you?"

She swallowed. "I..."

He sat back, laying both hands flat on the table. "You're such a damn coward about some things. Just answer me. *Aren't* you?"

Cat stared at him, as she admitted to herself that talking, really, was the last thing she wanted to do. She slowly stood. "Look. I don't know what's happening here."

He made a low, disgusted sound. "The hell you don't."

Cat felt like a person who'd walked off the edge of an invisible cliff. She was falling, spiraling downward. And she hadn't even seen the place where the ground fell away.

For two weeks, she'd grown to know and like the Dillon McKenna who'd returned to Red Dog City after sixteen years in the big, wide world. She'd assumed that the young, wild Dillon she'd once known was long gone. That from the angry, dangerous boy he had been years ago, he'd matured into a good-humored, easygoing man.

She'd been a fool. The danger was still there. How could she not have seen that? A leopard might be trained to walk around on a leash, but it was still a leopard. And anyone who dealt with it would be worse than an idiot to forget that fact.

She stared into his upturned face. The little scar on his lip stood out whitely against his bronze skin. His dark eyes bored through her, staggering in their intensity. His breathing was careful, deliberate. Measured.

"Sit back down," he said. "And we'll have this out."

He *was* like a leopard. A leopard about to pounce.

She knew beyond a shadow of a doubt that she had to get out of there. She squared her shoulders.

"This is pointless. I'm leaving." She turned and took a step toward the door.

That step was as far as she got. Dillon was out of his chair with a swiftness that belied all his artificial joints. He grabbed her shoulder and spun her around, knocking her off-balance.

She fell with a startled gasp against his hard, broad chest.

"Dillon?" Her fingers dug into his hard arms. She stared up at him in bewilderment.

"Cat." And his mouth came down and closed over hers.

Five

Cat was melting.

Her whole body was going liquid. It was appalling. It was wonderful. Dillon's mouth seduced hers, nibbling, nudging.

She heard herself groan. And then she allowed her lips to part. His tongue slid inside, slick and hot. He made a groaning sound, too, as his tongue teased and taunted her.

Cat couldn't believe this was happening.

She felt as if her legs were giving out on her—her good, strong, legs. They were as weak as a baby's legs, suddenly. She had to slide her hands up Dillon's chest and then grab his shoulders to remain on her feet.

Dillon kept her from falling. He held her tighter. His hands roamed her back, pressing her hard against him, as his tongue shamelessly explored her mouth.

For a moment, she pulled away. Enough to stare up, lost, into his eyes and try to tell him, "Dillon, I didn't..."

But then he made a low, growling sound. His mouth claimed hers again. His tongue delved in. And the melting continued, more intense than before.

His hands held her at the waist. And then they moved lower, sliding, hot and grasping, over the curve of her hips. He cupped her buttocks, bringing her up and against him. She gasped into his mouth as she felt that—felt *him*.

Never in her life had she—

The thought turned to ashes and blew away. She had no thoughts. She was what she had sworn never to be.

Woman and needful. Melting in a man's arms.

Very slowly, as he continued his assault on her mouth, he rubbed himself against her, holding her close and high, so she could feel that he wanted her.

He wanted her.

The thought came screaming out of the chaos that was her mind. Frightening. Incredible. Impossible, but true.

Still holding her mouth captive, he loosened his demanding grasp on her hips. His hands trailed up over the sides of her waist. Slowly, tauntingly, he skimmed the outer curves of her breasts. Then he was touching her shoulders, briefly, a sliding caress. At last, he cupped her face.

"Cat." He released her mouth just long enough to breathe her name across her lips.

And then the kissing began again.

As he kissed her, he urged her back, into the living area, and over to one of those big, beige couches. He took her shoulders and guided her down, then lowered himself next to her, so they were sitting side by side. His tongue swept her mouth. And his hand was at the top button of her shirt. She felt the button give way.

And then his hand slid in, under the cup of her serviceable bra.

The touch of his hand on her naked breast stunned her. Her breast was a very soft part of her, and his hand felt rough in comparison. Rough and encompassing. He caught her nipple between two fingers and pressed it a little.

She cried out and arched her back against his palm.

His mouth slid over to her ear. "Yeah," he said in a hoarse whisper. "Move for me, Cat, show me what you want."

She gave another needful cry. He muttered more low, seductive encouragements.

And then he worked swiftly, slipping more buttons free so that her shirt fell open. His fingers set to roving, gliding down over her belly and the placket of her jeans to slip between her thighs.

He touched her there, at her most private place. His touch was warm and full of sensual promise, even through the layers of clothing that she wore.

He flicked her earlobe with his tongue, then bit it lightly. "It's been driving me nuts. Wondering when. Wondering how. Ever since that first day two weeks ago when I found you down in back of the house." His hand slid up again, and dipped inside her bra.

Cat jerked and sighed at the intimate contact. At the same time, her fogged mind slowly absorbed what he'd just told her. That he'd wanted her from the first day he came home. That what she'd sworn to herself was impossible was actually true.

Dillon McKenna had been after her.

He'd wanted to make love with her. From the first.

And he was going to make love with her. Right here and now. On this couch—if she didn't get a backbone from somewhere and call a halt to this.

He took her chin and guided it around so that she looked into his dazzling, heavy-lidded eyes. "Say you want me. I want to hear you say it. I want to end the pretense that you come here to work for me. I'm sick of that lie. We both know why you come here. Say it. Say it out loud."

She stared at him, her body aching for him, her mind a confused jumble of conflicting, half-formed thoughts.

"Say it, Cat. We'll start fresh from here."

Everything spun around in her head. Herself, as she lived, as she wanted to be. Free and unfettered, unclaimed by any man. Adora. The woman named Natalie Evans. And perhaps other women, who knew how many?

"Stop it," he commanded. His voice was harsh, guttural. "Stop thinking." His hand was tender, warm and tempting on her breast. He gently squeezed. "Except for this. Think about this."

"No..." The sound was so weak, it was more a sigh than a word.

"Say it. Admit you want me."

"I can't..."

"You can."

"No."

"Yes." He lowered his mouth to hers.

She wanted his kiss. She yearned for it.

But she couldn't let it happen. In the second before his lips touched hers, she turned her face away.

"Cat?"

She didn't answer.

"Don't turn away."

She said nothing.

He swore, low and crudely, and pulled away from her, withdrawing to the other end of the couch.

For several terrible seconds after that, Cat remained frozen, looking toward the stairs to the lower level, waiting for her heart to stop pounding so hard.

Then, as swiftly as she could with fingers that seemed numb, she buttoned up her shirt and tucked it back into her jeans. When she was decent, she turned to him.

He had collected himself, as she had. He lounged back against the armrest, watching her.

She rose on shaky legs and stood looking down at him.

He met her gaze. "Coward." The word was a cold caress.

"Say whatever you want. I'll never make love with you."

"*Never*'s one of those words that makes a man want to call your bluff."

"I'm not bluffing." She raised her chin a little higher. "You planned all this, didn't you?"

"Planned what?"

"Getting me here to work for you, *inventing* things for me to do."

He shrugged. "Yeah. I did. A lot of it anyway."

"What do you mean?"

"I mean I really did want all the bookshelves and the desk. But I broke the mirrors on purpose and it took me an hour of feeding that potato peeler into the disposal to mangle the cutting blades bad enough that you'd have to come over and replace it for me."

"But why?"

"Oh, come on, Cat. You're not stupid. What choice did I have? I was never going to get to know you better by asking you out on a date. I don't think you've ever even *been* on a date." He waited for her to insist that she had. But she couldn't, because he was right. After a minute, he went on, "So I needed an excuse to be around you for a while, before I suggested anything so *radical* as dinner, drinks and a show."

She still couldn't believe it. "But *why?* You could have *any* woman."

He smiled, a bleak curling of his lips. "I don't want *any* woman."

She didn't know what to say to that, so she pointed out as firmly as she could, "Well, you'll have to find someone other than me."

"Why?"

"A thousand reasons."

"I'll settle for one, if it's an honest one."

She scraped a hand back through her hair and held it there, pulling hard enough that she felt her scalp tighten. "One."

"Yeah. One."

"Because..." She let her hand drop to her side.

"You've said nothing."

"I'm getting there."

"I'm waiting."

She longed to turn and walk away. But she *had* returned his kisses and moved in yearning beneath his touch. She felt she owed him some kind of explanation.

"Any day now," he prompted silkily.

"Okay, okay." She inhaled and let it out slowly. Then she forged ahead. "Because...I run my own life and I have my freedom and I don't want that to change. Because I spent ten years raising my father's family for him after he died, so I've done my bit taking care of other people. Because now I have myself to look out for, and no one else, and that is how it's going to stay."

He looked her up and down, one of those slow, measuring looks she'd seen men give other women all the time—the kind of look no man had ever dared to try on her. She stood straight beneath his insolent inspection, hating her body for the way it seemed to soften and yearn.

Then he chuckled in a low, insulting way. "I said I wanted you, Cat. But I don't remember asking you for a lifetime commitment."

She refused to respond to those words in any way but reasonably. "No. You didn't. What you're asking for is *lovemaking*."

"That I'll admit to. I want to make love with you."

"Well, I don't want to make love with you."

"Liar."

"I don't want what it leads to."

"And what exactly is that?"

She cast about for the right word—and found it. "Entanglements. I don't want entanglements."

"What is that supposed to mean?"

She snorted disdainfully. "Just what it sounded like. Entanglements. Involvements. And feelings...useless, fluttery, energy-absorbing feelings. I don't need *any* of that. I don't need it one little bit."

He stood then.

She backed up a step.

But he closed the distance. She decided to hold her ground at that point, and looked at him defiantly, her eyes promising dire consequences should he dare to touch her.

He didn't, but his voice seemed to reach out and stroke her nonetheless. "Aw, Cat. Give those feelings a chance. You may say you don't need them, but you sure as hell seem to like them."

She stepped back again. "No."

"Cat."

She put up a hand. "Leave me alone. I mean it."

"If you say that too many times, I just might believe you."

"Believe me. I do mean it."

Suddenly he looked sad. "It takes two, Cat. To make it happen."

"That's what I'm telling you. It's not going to happen. From now on, you just call someone else when you need a hand around the house." There was a silence. He went on looking at her, that strange sadness in his eyes. She demanded, "Do you understand?"

"Yeah. You're coming through loud and clear."

"Goodbye, then."

He said nothing. She ordered her body to turn away from him and her rubbery legs to take her to the door.

"Cat?"

She stopped, her hand on the door latch.

"Before you go, there's something I want *you* to understand."

"What?" She didn't turn.

He said quietly, "You wouldn't let me tell you about Natalie. But there's one thing I *will* say. There's nothing between Adora and me. That was years ago. We were only kids. It ended for good the day I left town."

Cat gripped the door latch tighter, but somehow her arm wasn't taking the signal from her brain. The door remained shut.

"Cat."

She felt so weak then, a weakness all through her, the likes of which she'd never known before. She leaned her forehead against the door. "I don't need to hear this."

"Yes, you do. Because I know you love your sister. And you're loyal as hell. You'd do just about anything for someone you loved. And I believe you have some crazy idea that if I can't have you, I'll turn to Adora."

Cat made herself step back from the door. She gave it a yank and the door swung inward. The cold winter air was like a brisk slap in the face.

"Cat. Did you hear me?"

"I heard you. And it doesn't matter. That's between you and Adora."

Cat spent the rest of the day checking on the houses that she took care of for the real estate agency. When she got home, it was twilight and a gentle snow was falling. She threw a sandwich together and ate it standing at the sink.

Once she'd eaten, she went out to her shop by the woodshed and worked until very late on Dillon's desk. She wanted to get it finished and delivered to him as soon as possible. She wanted no loose ends between them.

The next day was Sunday. Cat visited the community church in town but found little comfort there. When she got home, she worked all afternoon and evening on the desk. She finished it at 2:00 a.m. on Monday. Then she managed to sleep for a few hours.

When she woke, the sun was bright on the new layer of white outside. Cat called Bob Tamberlaine, since she knew it was one of the two mornings a week that Bob worked for Dillon. Bob agreed to stop by on his way to clean Dillon's house. Between the two of them, Cat and Bob hauled the finished desk outside and hefted it into the back of Cat's pickup.

Bob followed her to Dillon's, where he helped her get the desk out of the pickup and inside to the study downstairs. Once it was in place, Dillon declared it to be exactly what he'd wanted, big and rustic and stained a warm, blond color. Though she didn't want to react to him in any way, Cat couldn't suppress the flush of pleasure she felt from his praise.

Next, Dillon sat down at his new desk and wrote out a very large check for the price of the new piece of furniture as well as the second of the two weeks Cat had worked for him. As he wrote, Cat took the keys to his house and garage off of her key ring.

"I guess we're even, then," he said. They traded—the money for the keys.

"Yes." She forced a distant smile and was careful not to let his hand brush hers as the switch was accomplished.

Bob, who was wielding a long-handled feather duster out in the adjacent central room, stuck his head in the door. "Hey. Did you check out that smell from the kitchen? Lunch is going to be something. You oughtta hang around."

For some ridiculous reason, Cat wanted to cry. And she *never* cried. "No. I have to get going." She forced herself to face Dillon again. He was watching her with a closed expression on his face.

The most disturbing thought occurred to her.

She was going to *miss* him.

She hadn't truly realized that he had become a friend until she'd cut herself off from him. And now she did realize it.

But what choice did she have? He wanted more than friendship. And that sort of thing just wasn't for her.

"I...um..."

"I think goodbye is the word." His voice was flat.

"Yes. Goodbye."

She made herself wave and smile at Bob as she went out.

* * *

After that, Cat discovered something new in her life: loneliness. Her solitude had no peace in it. The quiet of her isolated little house no longer gave her satisfaction.

It made her crazy instead.

She took to watching television at night because the books that had always been her refuge required too much concentration. For the next few days, her evenings began with "Wheel of Fortune," progressed through "Jeopardy" and "Entertainment Tonight" and spun out into sitcoms and movies of the week.

More than once, she actually fell asleep in front of the television and woke staring at the flickering screen, wondering where she was. Eventually she became so disgusted with herself that she decided she just had to get out of the house one of these nights soon.

The next day, she ran into Lizzie Spooner at the Superserve Mart.

"Adora and I are having a girls' night out," Lizzie said. "Tonight. About eight at the Spotted Owl." The Spotted Owl was Red Dog City's one night spot. "You ought to drop in. It may turn into a real party. Adora invited Dillon. And Bobby Tamberlaine said he might come, too."

As soon as she heard that Dillon might be there, Cat knew she wouldn't go. But when evening came around, she began to think that anything—even facing Dillon again—was preferable to falling asleep in front of another rerun of "Baywatch."

Cat arrived at the tavern at 8:40 that night. But the minute she stepped inside the place, Cat knew she'd been kidding herself. True, Dillon was nowhere in sight, so she didn't have to worry about dealing with him.

But the Spotted Owl Tavern on a weeknight in the middle of winter made another evening of television reruns look more attractive by the minute.

Though the restaurant next door was rather cozy, the tavern itself couldn't be called anything but dreary. It was dim and smoky; all the lit-up beer signs hardly pierced the gloom. And most of the customers were local men with no wives to go home to. They sat at the bar, nursing long necks and staring glumly at their own reflections in the mirror over the bar.

Lizzie and Adora were there, sitting at a table in the middle of the room. A couple of tattooed biker types lurked nearby, pretending to play pool, but really gearing up to move in on the only two female customers in the place.

Cat took one look and realized this was the last place she wanted to be. She started to turn and march right back out the door.

But Lizzie had seen her. "Hey, Cat! Over here!"

Reluctant to just leave now that she'd been spotted, Cat decided she'd have one beer before heading home again. Calling greetings to several of the men she knew, she stopped at the bar and had Bernice, the owner and bartender, pour her a draft. Then she joined the other two women, taking the empty chair next to her sister's.

"Hey, stranger," Adora said in a voice that seemed falsely bright. "Where have you been keeping yourself?"

Cat wasn't sure how to answer. It was true that Cat had been avoiding Adora, but Adora hadn't called her in quite a while, either. And it had been weeks since the last time Adora had strolled in Cat's kitchen door without bothering to knock. In Cat's opinion, avoidance was the order of the day on both sides.

"I've been really busy." Cat knocked back a mouthful of beer as soon as the unimaginative lie was out of her mouth.

"Doing what?" Adora asked, still in that brittle tone.

Cat was spared having to think up another lie because right then, one of the two guys who'd been lurking by the pool table stuck his head between Cat and Adora.

"How would you three sweet babes like a little music?" Grinning widely, he looked from Adora to Lizzie and then to Cat. He had huge biceps. The tatoo on the arm that Cat could see was of a boa constrictor squeezing the blood out of a heart.

Adora gave him a strained smile. "Music would be nice."

"Whoa, baby, you're a pretty one." He wrapped a massive arm around her and blew in her ear.

Adora angled back. "Thanks. Why don't you go and play the music?"

He pulled her closer. "Why don't you come on over there with me? You can pick out the tunes."

"I...I can't. I'm with my friend. And my sister here." Adora gestured weakly in Cat's direction. Cat wondered what it was about Adora that made it so difficult for her to tell a creep to take a hike.

"Your sister won't mind, will she?" The man swung around and smirked at Cat, though he kept his arm around Adora.

Cat didn't share Adora's reluctance to offend, especially not tonight, when her nerves were on edge anyway. She looked the tattooed giant up and down. "What's your name, anyway?" She tried to inject the question with just as much loathing as she felt.

But the biker didn't seem to pick up on nuances. He only grinned wider. His back molars were silver. "My name's Spike. What's yours?"

She let a moment elapse before she answered in a voice thick with disgust, "Cat."

The biker went on grinning. "Well, Cat. Do you mind if I take your pretty sister here over to the jukebox to choose a few tunes?"

Cat drank from her beer again, then carefully set it down. She swallowed. "Well, Spike. It's like this. My sister's too polite to tell you, but she'd rather have root canal surgery than stroll over to that jukebox with you."

Spike couldn't quite seem to take that in. He tried a smarmy laugh. "Naw..."

"Yes. Take your hand off her."

Spike grunted and pulled Adora closer. He was starting to get the idea that Cat wasn't friendly. "Whose gonna make me?"

Adora groaned. "Look. Can't we—?"

"Shut up, you sweet thing," Spike instructed. "I'm talkin' to your sister here—at least I *thought* she was your sister, but maybe she's your brother instead." Spike glanced over his shoulder at his buddy for a little moral support. "Ain't that so, Dooley?"

Dooley guffawed. "Yeah, Spike. Maybe it's her brother. It just might be. But then, she's got an awful cute little butt on her. For a *brother,* I mean..."

That did it for Adora. "All right. Enough." She shoved away from Spike, who let her go because he hadn't expected she'd dare to resist him.

"Hey, where d'ya think you're goin'?" Spike grabbed for her again.

Adora lurched back, knocking her chair over. "Leave me alone!"

"Hey, you guys," Lizzie, safe on the other side of the table, piped up nervously, "maybe you oughtta—"

"Come back here, sweet thing," Spike insisted in a menacing drawl. "You could get me mad if you run away from me. And gettin' me mad ain't good for anybody." He took a step toward Adora.

Cat stuck out her boot and Spike went crashing to the floor.

"Hey! No fights in here! Take it outside!" Bernice hollered from behind the bar.

Cat stood.

A friend at the bar called, "You need some help, Cat?"

Cat waved and shook her head. Slowly she approached the fallen Spike, who had already rolled and come up into a crouch.

"As I said," Cat patiently told him, "my sister would rather have a melanoma removed than go anywhere with flotsam like you."

Clearly Spike didn't know what a melanoma was—nor flotsam, for that matter. But he was pretty sure they weren't that good.

"Okay, you..." Spike called Cat a distinctly unflattering name. "You asked for it. You wanna strut around like a man, you're gonna take it like a man."

"Oh, no. Don't!" Adora wailed. "Cat, tell him you're sorry."

Cat had no intention of doing any such thing. She felt reckless. All her confusion and unhappiness over what had happened with Dillon seemed to be driving her toward something crazy. She was trouble looking to happen and here was a perfect opportunity to work off some frustration.

"All right, Spike," Cat said. "Just step right up here and—"

"Have a tall one on me." The deep, warm voice came from directly behind Cat.

Spike's face went slack. "Well, I'll be damned."

"Dillon!" Adora clapped her hands in glee and relief. "Thank goodness you're here."

Cat whirled.

And there he was, looking her up and down and smiling his slow, rakish smile. Cat felt it: that despised, womanly weakness, loosening her spine and heating up her belly.

Behind Cat, Spike mused in awe, "It's *the* Dillon McKenna. Tell me I ain't dreamin', Dooley."

"You're wide-awake, Spike," Dooley breathed reverently. "It's Dillon McKenna, sure enough."

Dillon stepped around Cat and stuck out his hand. Spike took it, and Dillon pulled the other man to his feet.

"This is an honor, a freakin' honor," Spike said, shaking Dillon's hand for all he was worth. "I seen every jump you ever did, or at least all the ones they ran on 'Universe of Sports' and 'Real-Life Gladiators of the Twenty-first Century.'"

"Well, thank you." Dillon was modesty personified. "I truly thank you. It's the fans that made me what I am." He called to Bernice. "Drinks for everyone! On me!"

"You got it!" Bernice replied. She went right to work setting them up.

"Dooley. I'm Dooley." Spike's friend stuck out his beefy hand.

Dillon shook it. "Pleased to meet you, Dooley." Then he put one arm around Dooley and one around Spike and hauled them off to the end of the bar where Bernice served them up their drinks and Dillon launched into some long story about how he once drove a truck through the roof of a barn.

Adora sighed. "Isn't he something?" Her dreamy gaze was glued to Dillon's broad back.

Cat ground her teeth together. "Yeah. He's a prize, all right."

"Cat." Adora's voice dripped rebuke. "How can you use that tone about Dillon? He's been nothing but good to you, since he came home. Giving you all that work. And look at what he did just now? Stepping in like that and saving you from—"

"I was handling myself just fine."

Adora gave a ladylike snort. "I beg your pardon. You were about to get beat up by some guy named Spike."

"Don't be so sure about that. I can handle myself."

Adora shook her head. "Honestly. What is with you lately?"

Your precious Dillon McKenna, that's what, Cat wanted to say. But she didn't. All her recklessness had left her. She felt like a helium balloon on the morning after, sadly deflated, dragging the floor.

"Oh, look, here are our drinks." Adora perked up and waved at Dillon. "Thanks, Dillon!"

Dillon gave her a high sign.

Cat righted Adora's chair. Then she picked up the fresh draft Bernice had set on the table in front of her own chair and drained it in one gulp.

She set the mug down. "Gotta go."

"But, Cat—" Lizzie started to protest.

Adora looked at Cat disdainfully. "No, Lizzie. Don't stop her. If she has to go, she has to go. She's not a lot of fun to have around lately anyway."

Cat stared at her sister, anger and misery and hurt fighting for the upper hand inside her.

She let none of her feelings show. She only said, "See you later," and headed for the door.

* * *

It was one-thirty the next morning before Cat admitted that she was never going to get any sleep that night. Every time she dropped off, she would relive the moment when she'd turned to face Dillon in the Spotted Owl Tavern.

She'd experience all over again that dreaded, womanly feeling of weakness, of surrender. And it would get worse. Because in her dream, she had no shame. In her dream, she would step forward and throw her arms around Dillon. He would chuckle at her hunger and her need.

And then he'd give her what she wanted: his mouth covering hers.

Cat moaned and sat up straight in bed. Then she tossed back the covers. She shivered, even in her long johns. The fires had burned down and her poorly insulated little house was already taking on the forbidding predawn chill.

Cat shoved her feet into a pair of jeans and pulled on two sweaters. She yanked on some heavy socks and laced up her boots. Her room was off the kitchen, so she went out the side door there, grabbing her coat and her keys as she went.

It was so cold that she let her pickup idle for a few minutes to warm it up a little. Then she headed out into the freezing heart of the night.

Her pickup seemed to know where to go, though she would have sworn that she'd never intended to head that way.

It was only two miles to Dillon's house. She was there in five minutes from the time she pulled out of her driveway.

Six

The floodlights in front of the house were on, casting wide, eerie swaths of brightness upward, toward the stars. But the few windows in front were dark, which wasn't terribly surprising this late at night.

Cat sat in her pickup for several minutes after she'd pulled into the driveway, wondering what she was doing here.

She'd heard about how lovesick women did things like this. Adora had told her all about it, since Adora herself was no stranger to lovesickness.

"It's the worst," Adora had moaned. "The absolute rock bottom. When you find yourself driving by his house in the middle of the night, a victim of your own reckless heart, looking to see if the lights are on, if there's a shadow on the shade. Wondering if he's maybe thinking of you. Or if he's with somebody else...."

Cat folded her hand into a fist and hit the dashboard hard enough to hurt. Then she slid out of the pickup and marched up to the porch.

Though she had absolutely no idea what she was going to do when Dillon answered, she pounded on the door and rang the bell. Then she waited. But nothing happened. She knocked and rang some more.

Several minutes later, when her knuckles were starting to hurt from knocking, she had to admit to herself that Dillon either wasn't there or wasn't going to answer.

As she turned from the house, she had an idea. She trudged through the snow to the side door of the garage and looked in the window at the top of the door. The fancy red Land Cruiser—which Dillon called a "truck," but which was really an oversize, sturdy four-wheel-drive station wagon—wasn't there.

Cat returned to her pickup, started it up and drove out to the road again. When she reached the turnoff to her house, she passed it by. She drove on to the highway that would take her to town.

She needed some company, she decided. But where could she go to find someone to talk to? The dashboard clock said it was after two now. The Spotted Owl would be closed.

And then Cat realized what she'd do. She'd go see Adora. She'd give her sister a chance to pay her back for all those nights when Adora had been the one needing someone to talk to and that someone had always been Cat. Just maybe, tonight, Cat was disturbed enough in her mind to have it out with her sister, to talk to Adora of the hard things: of Dillon and these new feelings she was having. Of where it all might lead, if Cat were to give it a chance.

Cat shivered at the thought of how Adora might react. She knew her sister wouldn't be pleased. But maybe, with love and honesty, they could start to work it out.

As soon as she reached Bridge Street, Cat began scanning the curb for a likely place to park. She saw several places. And she also saw Dillon's red Land Cruiser, parked directly in front of the Shear Elegance Salon of Beauty.

Cat came to a stop right in the middle of the street. She looked up at the windows above the salon. The lights were on in her sister's apartment.

Were Dillon and Adora alone together up there?

Cat scanned the street again, her heart knocking painfully against her ribs. She searched frantically for Lizzie Spooner's little compact car. Or Bob Tamberlaine's van. She saw neither.

Cat rested her forehead on the steering wheel, wanting to curse, wanting to cry out loud. She felt that someone had taken her heart and tied it in a double knot.

She wanted to pull over into one of those vacant parking slots and get out of her pickup. She wanted to march up Adora's back stairs and find out the truth about what was going on up there.

But she knew she wouldn't do that. She'd told Dillon that she would never make love with him. And though he'd insisted he wouldn't turn to Adora, the man had a right to change his mind. Adora was free and so was he.

Coward, Dillon had called her. And he had been so very right. There might be any number of explanations for what Dillon was doing at Adora's tonight, but Cat didn't want to know them.

It was just too hurtfully confusing, this thing that went on between women and men.

Cat took her foot off the brake and drove on down the street. She was going home. There would be no more of this foolishness for her. It might take her a month of sleepless nights, but she'd get over Dillon McKenna. And her life would be as it had been once more.

Cat didn't even bother to go to bed when she got home. She turned on the television and sat on the couch wrapped in a blanket, waiting for daybreak. Eventually she dozed off. She woke, freezing, to daylight and the cheerful morning weatherman announcing that a doozy of a storm was moving in.

Cat built up the fires again. Then, longing for a cup of coffee, she grabbed the carafe to her automatic coffeemaker and heedlessly shoved it under the faucet to fill it with water. It slammed against the side of the sink, shattering with an explosive pop and raining glass everywhere. Cat stared down at the mess, her hands clutching the edge of the sink in a death grip.

"It's only a coffeepot," she muttered tightly to herself.

So why did she want to throw her head back and wail out loud?

Well, whatever the reason, she would not do that. She would not give in to a foolish, emotional outburst over nothing at all.

She gritted her teeth and cleaned up the mess.

By ten, she'd made her rounds of the houses she took care of, checking to be sure each was secured against the predicted heavy snows. As the sky darkened overhead, she drove into town to pick up milk and eggs and a loaf of bread at the Superserve Mart. If the storm was as bad as the weatherman had promised, she could be snowed in for a day or two.

As an afterthought, she stopped at Kratt's Hardware Store in the far-flung hope that old Reggie Kratt might have a replacement on hand for her coffee carafe. No such luck.

"You could buy a whole new machine," Reggie suggested, pointing at the shelf where he kept his small appliances.

"No, thanks. I'll pick up a new carafe the next time I'm in Reno."

Not to be done out of a sale, the cagey old store owner brandished an old-fashioned aluminum percolator at her.

"Anyway, what the hell do you need with one of them fancy coffeemakers, Cat? You buy this coffeepot here, it'll last a lifetime and more."

"No, thanks, Reggie. I've already got one of those."

"Well, then, put it to use and forget that newfangled, useless gadget, okay?"

"I'll give it some thought," Cat promised dryly.

The old man chortled. "That means 'Mind your own business, Reggie.' Am I right?"

"Well . . ."

Cat shivered a little as someone opened the door behind her and a blast of cold air came in from outside.

"Hey there, Dillon." Reggie cackled. "What's up?"

Cat felt it: the weakness, the longing. Her knees turned to rubber. Though she hadn't even moved, her heart pounded deep and hard, as if she were running the last mile of a marathon.

Dillon came right up to the counter and stood beside her. "Hello, Cat." His voice was nothing more nor less than polite. His eyes were flat.

She forced a tight smile. "Hello, Dillon."

He turned to Reggie. "I got to thinking I could use a few kerosene lanterns with the storm coming in. Just in case the electricity goes out."

"Now those, I got," Reggie answered proudly. "Down that far aisle there, near the back wall. Got kerosene?"

"Yeah, five gallons of it at home."

"Good then. What else can I do you for?"

"That's it. I'm heading over to Reno for groceries, want to get stocked up before—"

"What's the matter with you, boy?" Reggie demanded. "Ain't you looked at that sky out there? If you go to Reno, you stay there until this mess that's rollin' in blows over."

Dillon laughed, that rich, deep laugh that made the back of Cat's knees tingle and set a bunch of fluttery things loose inside her belly. "I'll be fine, Reggie. I've got snow tires and four-wheel drive—and chains, too, if it comes to that."

"You've got a head full of rocks, if you try to race this here storm."

Cat agreed with Reggie. She opened her mouth before she realized that what she should be doing was getting out of there. "Dillon, Reggie's right. Maybe you ought to wait until—"

He swung his dark gaze her way. He didn't smile. "I appreciate your concern, Cat." He stressed the word *concern* as if they both knew it was the last thing she'd ever feel for him. "But I can take care of myself."

Cat stared at him. His words had been as harsh as a slap in the face.

Dillon looked at Reggie. "Now, where did you say those lanterns were?"

Reggie pointed and Dillon went to find the lanterns.

"Er, anythin' else you need, Cat?" Reggie was looking at her uncomfortably. He was a sharp old coot. He knew as well as she did that Dillon McKenna had just cut her dead.

"No, no, that's all." Cat forced her numb legs to turn her around and take her to the door. "You take care of yourself, Reggie."

"You bet. Same to you."

An hour and a half after Cat arrived home, the wind started howling and the snow began to fall.

Around three, the phone rang. It was Adora, wanting to know if Cat was all right, saying she'd closed up her shop and was all settled in to weather the storm.

"Are you okay there?" Adora asked.

Cat felt a surge of warmth for her sister. Whatever distances lay between them since Dillon McKenna had returned to town, it was good to have someone in her life who cared enough to check on her when a storm was moving in.

"Yeah. I'm fine. Plenty of wood. And candles and kerosene. I could last a week without leaving this house."

"Well, I hope you won't have to."

"Me, too."

There was a silence. The line crackled with static from the storm.

Then Adora spoke hesitantly, "Cat, I..."

Suddenly Cat was gripping the receiver too tightly. "Adora? What?"

There was more crackling on the line. Then a nervous laugh from Adora. "Oh, nothing. Listen. Stay safe, will you? And keep warm."

Cat promised she would.

A half an hour later, the electricity went out. The snow was coming down so thick that it seemed like night inside the house. The wind whistled and moaned around the eaves.

Cat already had the candles and lanterns ready. She lit them in the kitchen and the living room and filled the small spaces with the cozy glow that only light from a flame creates.

Cat tried not to worry about Dillon. She had absolutely no right or reason to be doing that. As he'd so coldly pointed out to her, he could take care of himself. And perhaps when the snow started coming down, he had reconsidered and spent the night in Reno after all.

In any case, she was not going to call his house just to see that he'd made it home all right. She absolutely was not.

Yet somehow, Cat found herself punching out his number not five minutes after she'd sworn to herself she wouldn't.

She listened, her hands shaking a little, through four rings. Then his machine picked it up and Dillon's recorded voice advised her to leave a message. Her throat closed up, as she imagined him standing over his answering machine, screening his calls for just such an eventuality as this.

But her pride lost out to concern for his safety. She forced herself to speak. "Dillon. It's Cat. It's really coming down bad over here. I'm kind of worried about you, since you said you were going to Reno today. If you're there, would you please pick up?"

Cat waited. Nothing happened, except for the line popping and scratching from the storm.

She tried again. "Please, Dillon. Let me know you're all right. Pick up the phone and tell me to mind my own business and then hang up. But will you please just let me know you're all right?''

But he didn't. If he was there, the man had a heart of stone.

Her face flaming, Cat put the receiver back in its cradle. She tried to be mad at him, for not picking up, for standing there listening to her and making her squirm.

But she couldn't even convince herself to be angry. She knew it would only be a way of hiding from her fear for his safety. Because, in spite of the cold way he'd spoken to her at the hardware store, Cat didn't for a minute believe Dillon McKenna had a heart of stone.

Which meant he wasn't home. That he was very likely out on the road somewhere in what seemed to be shaping up into the worst blizzard in years.

Cat paced from the living room to the kitchen and back again, telling herself to stop worrying, that Dillon was fine, really, probably in Reno, in some fancy hotel. She just had to let it go, stop worrying about it, since there was absolutely nothing she could do.

She was staring out the window in the living room at a wall of white, thinking that she couldn't even see the twin spruce trees ten feet from the porch, when, for the briefest of seconds, she saw a flash of red.

Not even realizing she was holding her breath, she craned forward and pressed her nose against the glass.

Yes. There it was. Red. Shiny red metal. A flash, and then covered again by the swirling storm. But it had looked as if it were a vehicle, a *red* vehicle, pulling into her driveway at the side of the house.

With a small, urgent cry she didn't even know she'd made, Cat ran for the kitchen and the door that opened onto a side porch and her driveway. She flung back the door, heedless of the wind and driving snow.

The red Land Cruiser was right there, parked beside the porch. It was real. She could see it, here in the lee of the house, where the storm wasn't so wild. Dillon hooked his legs over the console and switched to the passenger side. Then he opened the door.

"I was too scared to keep going," he said, shouting a little to compete with the wind. "I was afraid I might not make it the final two miles to my place. And not only that, I—"

Inside her chest, her heart was galloping. It was freezing and she'd stepped out without a coat. She could see absolutely no reason to stand here in a blizzard and talk about why he'd stopped at her house. The reason was obvious. It was too dangerous to go on. She cut him off before he could say more. "You did the right thing. Hurry. Come in."

He swung his legs out and slid down from the vehicle. And then, though the storm pressed in on them from beyond the Land Cruiser and the porch, both stood still. They looked at each other, struck simultaneously with what his stopping here meant. They would spend this night at least, and probably longer, alone together in her small house.

Cat was conscious of his warmth and his size. And of her longing for him, that seemed so much a part of her now that she could hardly remember what it had been like before she felt it.

She shivered, but not really with cold. "Come in. Please," she said, bowing her head a little. She felt awkward again, and hid behind formality.

"I will. But first, I . . ." He seemed not to know how to go on.

She searched his face. "What?"

He looked away, then back. "I have some . . . things in the back. Groceries and things. They'll freeze if I—"

"I understand. Let me get my jacket and I'll help you bring them in." She started to turn.

He grabbed her arm. "No. Wait."

She looked up at him, bewildered. "Dillon. What is it?"

"Hell," he said grimly. "Just wait here." And then he spun on his heel and marched down the porch to the back of the Land Cruiser. He stepped off onto the driveway, which was like stepping off the edge of the world. For a moment, he disappeared.

Cat stood by the door to her kitchen, holding herself tight against the cold.

At last, he reappeared and Cat blinked when she saw him.

He was carrying a bundle wrapped in a fluffy pink blanket. Cat realized it was a baby when she heard its angry wail.

Seven

Dillon marched up to her. "I think it's a *she,* since everything is pink." From inside the pink blanket, the angry cries continued as a gust of frigid wind blew down the porch.

Cat clutched her arms tighter around herself. "What is going on, Dillon?"

"Well, I . . ." He looked at her, a rueful look that said he hadn't a clue where to begin. In his arms, the baby sucked in a big breath and let out a real doozy of a wail. Dillon looked down at it. "Hey, hey, don't do that. . . ." He jiggled the poor thing, too roughly.

Cat held out her arms. "Give her to me."

Looking immensely relieved, Dillon handed over the bundle. A bottle fell out. He managed to catch it before it hit the porch. "Here. I'll get the groceries."

Cat took the bottle. "Fine." She turned for the warmth of the house.

She went straight to her bedroom and set the child on the bed. The fussing and crying immediately intensified; the little one hadn't wanted to be put down.

Cat turned swiftly and lit the two candles she'd set on her dresser earlier, as well as the kerosene lantern she'd put beside the bed. By the time she bent over the baby again, the child had kicked her blanket away. Her little arms and feet, encased in a pink blanket sleeper, flailed angrily. Cat scooped her up, tucked the blanket around her once more and held her close.

"Hey, there. Settle down, now," Cat cooed softly.

The baby quieted a little, enough to open sapphire blue eyes and study Cat with solemn interest. Her pink mouth fell open a little, in a sort of dazed concentration. Cat smiled down at her, thinking of her two younger sisters. Deirdre had been born when Cat was ten, Phoebe one year later. Cat had helped change their diapers and fix their bottles. Sometimes, late at night, Cat used to get up with them to give her mother a rest.

The baby started to whimper again.

"What's the problem here, huh? A full diaper, maybe?"

As if she understood the question, the little face screwed up tight once more and another long wail ensued.

"Gotcha. We need clean diapers." In the next room, Dillon had just come in the door, probably laden with grocery bags. Cat called to him. "I'll need the diaper bag!"

She heard the grocery bags crackle as he set them down. Then he came and stood in the door to her room. She watched as his gaze tracked her private space, taking everything in. Then he was looking at Cat again. "The what?"

"The diaper bag. She needs to be changed." The baby let out another angry yelp, as if to punctuate Cat's statement.

"A diaper bag," Dillon repeated rather blankly. "I'll look." He turned back to the kitchen.

For a moment after he was gone, Cat stared at the space where he'd been standing. She was thinking that he was going to have a lot of explaining to do, once the baby was comfortable and all of his precious groceries were inside.

The baby, displeased with being ignored, fussed and hiccuped. To soothe her until Dillon returned, Cat sat down over by the window, in the old rocker that had once been her great-grandmother's. Rocking gently, she cooed to the frustrated child some more.

"Is this it?"

Cat looked up to see Dillon in the doorway again, holding a pink, multizippered bag with little yellow appliquéd giraffes on it.

She nodded. "Set it there on the bed."

Dillon set the bag down and Cat stood and went to the bed, where she carefully laid the baby on her back. Then she reached for the bag. As she'd hoped, there were not only several disposable diapers, but there were also a few small toys, an extra bottle full of what appeared to be baby formula, a fresh blanket sleeper and a fold-up plastic changing pad.

"Okay, little one." Cat spread open the changing pad. "We'll take care of this problem pronto." She put the baby on the pad and then looked up to see that Dillon was still in the doorway, watching her as if she were performing some truly amazing feat. "What *are* you staring at?"

"You're good with babies." He shook his head. "You don't know what terrific news that is."

She gave him a suspicious look. "Why?" But before he could answer, she put up a hand. "Never mind. We'll talk about all this later. Get the rest of your things in from the truck."

"Good idea." He turned to leave her again.

She called after him. "And don't forget those lanterns you bought at Kratt's, okay? We can use them."

"Gotcha."

Cat unsnapped the soft blanket sleeper and pulled open the tabs of the diaper. She found no surprises. The baby *was* a girl. And she did need to be changed.

Cat completed the job, humming a tune she used to hum to Deirdre and Phoebe all those years ago. When she was done, she put the now-contented baby over her shoulder and took the extra bottle of formula into the kitchen to warm it a little.

Dillon came in with the lanterns just as she set a pan of water on the wood-burning half of the kitchen stove.

"That's everything," he said, putting the three tall boxes on the table. "Now, where's your phone?"

She pointed through the door to the living room. "In there, on the desk under the stairs."

He strode to it and picked up the receiver. She could see him through the doorway, as he listened, and then punched the plunger several times. He noticed her watching him.

"It's dead," he said.

An hour later, Dillon's groceries were put away in Cat's cupboards, the baby was sleeping in a nest of pillows on Cat's bed and Dillon and Cat were sitting in the living room, sipping cups of percolated coffee and munching on sandwiches to silence their growling stomachs. The power was still out and the phone lines remained dead. Outside, night approached, though the snow was still coming down so thickly that it was difficult to tell the time of day.

Dillon sat on the couch and stared out the front window as if there were actually something to see but their own dim reflections in the glow of the lamps.

"I've lived in L.A. too long," he said quietly. "I'd forgotten how it can get up here. We could be stuck in this house for days if this keeps up."

Cat swallowed the last bite of her sandwich. "Yes." The word was curt. They had a much more pressing subject to discuss than how long they might be snowed in. She toed off the moccasins she wore around the house and tucked her legs up beside her in her big easy chair.

Dillon looked at her and sighed. "Okay. Hit me with it."

She straightened her shoulders. "I will. Where did that baby come from?"

Dillon scrubbed a hand down his face.

Cat grew edgy, waiting for him to answer. She heard herself blurt out, "Is it Natalie Evans's?"

He gaped at her for a count of three, his expression so comically nonplussed that she almost laughed. But then *he* was the one laughing—a low, rolling chuckle.

"Why is that so funny?"

"Oh, hell." The chuckle was winding down.

"Oh, hell, what?"

He took in a breath. "It's nothing. You'd just have to know Natalie, that's all. She's the last person in the world who'd be having a baby—let alone *losing* one."

Cat frowned, confused by her own conflicting urges. She wanted to know more about Natalie, though she shouldn't be wanting any such thing. But she knew that finding out where the baby had come from was what mattered right now.

She stuck to the main point. "Well then. If the baby doesn't belong to Natalie Evans, then whose is it?"

"I haven't the faintest idea."

"Excuse me?"

"I said I haven't a clue." He leaned forward, bracing his forearms on his knees. "It was like this. I drove into Reno and went to the supermarket. When I came out, the snow had started. So I headed for the highway, wanting to get back. But then I saw I was low on gas. So I stopped at one of those big, plaza-type gas stations. You know the kind, with a convenience store attached?"

"Yes, I know."

"While the tank was filling, I went inside to the rest room."

"What's this got to do with the baby?"

"Settle down, Cat. I'm getting there. I went inside. I used the toilet. And when I came out, I paid for my gas. Then I left. And that's all I can figure."

"Exactly what is it that you figure?"

"That while I was in the john, someone put that baby in the back of my Land Cruiser. Because she wasn't there when I left the supermarket. And that trip to the rest room was the only time I left the truck after that until I got here. I drove straight through.

"It was hell. Like driving through packing popcorn. I could hardly see a thing. I was crawling, I tell you. It took me three hours to get to Red Dog City and I knew I should probably stop there. But I really wanted to get on home, so I headed up on the state route. It was after I turned off onto Barlin Creek Road, about a mile from here, that the baby started crying."

He shook his head. "I gotta tell you, it was the weirdest thing. I'm inching along, wondering if I'm gonna be stranded, when all of a sudden, there's this whimpering sound from behind me."

Dillon sat back against the couch cushions again. "I was spooked. I almost drove into a snowbank. But somehow I kept on the road. After my heart stopped pounding so hard I couldn't hear myself think, I realized what had happened. I'd picked up a passenger—an extremely *young* passenger. It occurred to me that this was going to be a problem I could use some help with. So I started looking for the driveway to your place. God knows how I found it, but I did."

He picked up his coffee cup from the side table at his elbow and drank from it. "The rest you know."

Cat just looked at him for a moment. Then she asked, "But why? Why would someone do such a thing?"

"Beats me. And until the phone works again, we're unlikely to find out."

Cat said nothing. She was trying to decide whether to believe him or not. Her expression must have said as much because Dillon swore softly.

"Oh, come on, Cat. I did not kidnap that baby. Okay, so I haven't always been totally up-front with you. But breaking mirrors and jamming garbage disposals is the limit of my underhandedness, I swear. Do you actually believe I'm the kind of man who'd abduct an innocent child?"

"No," she said quietly after thinking a moment more. "I don't believe you'd steal a baby. Your explanation makes more sense than anything else I could imagine."

"Well, that's a relief to hear." His voice was heavy with irony.

"But the major question remains—who *would* do such a terrible thing to a helpless child?"

"As I said, we're not getting an answer to that one in the near future, not with both the power and phone out and the roads impassable."

They lapsed into silence. Outside, the wind roared. Finally, he asked, "So what next?"

Cat met his gaze. A thousand more questions—personal questions—begged to be asked. But she was afraid to give voice to them.

So she unfolded her legs and put her feet back in her moccasins. "I think my old baby cradle is upstairs somewhere. Let's go see if we can find it."

The cradle was stuck in the back of a low space under the eaves at the top of the stairs, a space that Cat had masked off with Sheetrock two years ago. Since then, she'd been using the space for storage. Hunched over and armed with a lantern, she maneuvered her way into the space.

The cradle was there, in the back, on top of a huge box that had once held a giant swamp cooler and now contained Lord knew what. Still hunched, since it was too cramped to stand, Cat lifted the lantern.

The shadows in the long, low space rose and danced. The old-fashioned Shaker-style cradle bounced into sharp relief, its shadow elongated and eerie against the far wall. Outside, the wind howled and moaned.

"Cat?" Dillon called from the room beyond.

"Yes. I've found it. It's here." She carefully set down the lantern on a dusty end table and squeezed her way back to where the cradle was waiting.

Moments later, she emerged. "Here we go." She placed the cradle, like a trophy, at Dillon's feet and went back for the lantern, reappearing right away. "Let's have a look at it."

She knelt easily. Dillon sank beside her a little more slowly. Lightly he touched the side of the cradle. It rocked gently, making the old floorboards beneath it squeak once or twice.

Cat watched the cradle rock. "My dad made it for me. Before I was born."

Dillon moved the lantern over a little, so the light bathed the small footboard. "Obviously."

She shot him a glance. "Obviously what?"

He pointed. "Obviously he made it before you were born."

Cat looked where Dillon pointed. As she knew it would be, her name, Catherine, was painted on the footboard with a simple little rosebud growing out of the ending *e*. But over the years, the paint had faded and worn away. Beneath her name, quite clearly, she could read the words Mitchell, Jr.

"Well." With diffident fingers, she touched the name beneath *her* name. "Pentimento."

Dillon looked from the faded words to her face. "What?"

"It's an artist's term."

"Meaning?"

"Meaning when an artist changes his mind, and paints over something in his painting with something else. Then, later, over the years, the original image fades through. When that ghostly image shows through, it's called pentimento. I think it's from Latin, meaning 'repent,' because the artist 'repented' his original choice."

Dillon was watching her. She didn't like the look on his face. "So, from the first, your old man planned that you'd be a boy. A little Mitchell, Jr."

Cat coughed and stood. "Yes, well. But I wasn't."

He looked up at her. "Exactly. You weren't."

She stiffened at his tone. "What do you mean by that?"

"Just what I said." He put his hand on the top stair rail and used it to help him stand. "No matter how much your father would have liked you to be a boy, you *weren't* a boy."

"That's pretty self-evident."

"Is it?"

Cat glared at him, extremely irritated at how smug and knowing he looked. Up until this moment, in spite of everything, they'd been getting along pretty well. But now she felt her anger rising. She ordered it down, though she couldn't bury it completely. Her voice was cold when she spoke.

"I hate it when people ask vague questions instead of saying what they mean."

"Should I be more specific?"

"Yes." He seemed to loom over her, much too close. She backed up a step, reconsidering the answer she'd just given him. "No." Quickly she turned away. "Forget it."

He dared to grab her arm.

Cat gasped and whipped her head around to look at him.

And she remembered that first day. By the wall of windows at his house. He'd grabbed her arm then, too.

And, looking back, it seemed that from that moment, everything in her life had started going wrong.

"Let me go," she demanded, just as she had that first day.

But this time, instead of letting go, he only said, "In a minute."

She gasped again, at the feel of his hand on her—and at his unmitigated gall.

"Maybe this damn blizzard is the best thing that could have happened for us," he said.

"You are crazy."

"Maybe so. But I'm here. And you're stuck with me for a while. And before this is over, you're going to have to deal with me."

"Don't bet on it."

"Is that a challenge? Hey, I always love a damn challenge. Ask L. W. Creedy. He'll tell you about me."

"Let *go* of my arm."

He pretended he didn't hear her, just went on talking as if she'd never said a word. "Did you ever stop to think, Cat, how much alike we are?"

She gave a little jerk, trying to yank her arm free; still, he held on. She was a strong woman, but he was stronger still. If he was determined to hold on to her, she was going to have to put up a real fight to even have a chance of getting away. She debated the wisdom of a fight—and as she debated she sneered at him. "We're not alike at all."

"Hell, yes. We are. Our fathers shaped us, defined who we grew up to be. Yours molded you to take the place of the son he never had. And then left you cold to fill his shoes."

"My father didn't *leave* me. My father died. He had a heart attack. It wasn't his fault."

"But you blame him."

"How dare you—"

"You do. You blame him. For leaving you with all those needy women to take care of. For taking away your chance at college, your chance to live your life as you'd dreamed it could be."

"No—"

He wasn't listening. "And *my* father. Hell, he makes yours look like a prize. What my father taught *me* was that my life was worth nothing. He got me by default because my mother died when I was two. My father never gave a damn for me. He told me more than once that I cramped his style, that he wished I'd never been born. Because of him, I hungered after dangerous risks to prove I was someone who mattered, not just Lonnie McKenna's worthless little loser of a kid.''

Dillon's words were hard to hear. Out of her anger rose sudden sympathy for the wounded child he had once been. For a moment, in her mind's eye, she saw him as a little boy, barefoot and dirty, sitting outside the Superserve Mart back when it was just plain old Red Dog City Grocery. He clutched a piece of jerky that some sympathetic adult had no doubt bought for him. He was gnawing on the stringy prize as if it were all he'd had to eat in days.

"You remember what I was," Dillon said harshly.

Cat looked into his eyes, saw the memory of hurt and shame there. "Dillon, I—''

He gripped her arm tighter. "Don't say it. Save your pity. I don't need it now. Where was I? Oh, yeah. We've taken on big challenges. You raised your father's family for him. I risked my fool neck every chance I got.''

"Dillon, please . . .''

"And we're both in our mid-thirties and still single. Both holding out against the real risks and challenges of living. Neither of us married. Neither with kids.''

She refused to buy that one. "Lots of people aren't married at our age. Look at Bob Tamberlaine. Lizzie Spooner. Adora.''

The minute Cat said her sister's name, she regretted it. So much of what she didn't want to talk about had to do with Adora.

Dillon knew that, of course. "Ah, Adora. A big chunk of the problem here. Not the whole problem by any means, but part of it. A start.''

"I don't want to talk about—"

He released her arm then, with an abrupt, angry swiftness. "Why is this not news to me? Of course you don't want to talk about Adora. You don't want to talk about anything, I know that. Not anything that will tear down the barriers between you and me." She started to walk away again. He spoke to her retreating back. "You'd rather make up things in your mind and tell yourself that a guy like me is nothing but trouble. That way you can feel justified in staying the hell away from me."

She couldn't let that pass. She whirled on him again. "That's not so," she argued, but the words were far from convincing, even to her own ears.

"Keep telling yourself that. Maybe someday you'll actually believe it. Hell, maybe you believe it now. But get this and get it good. There isn't a damn thing going on between Adora and me, except maybe friendship."

Cat snorted in disbelief at his nerve to utter such an outright lie. "Have you told Adora that?"

He nodded. "You bet I have."

That surprised her. It took her a minute before she managed to frame the word, "When?"

"Last night."

Cat stared at him as that information sank in. Last night she'd seen his truck at Adora's. "I, um... What time did you talk to Adora? And where were you when you talked to her?"

Dillon looked at her suspiciously, but then he shrugged. "I followed her to her place after the bar closed. We talked there. Why?"

There was an ancient straight chair a few feet away from Cat, beneath a window that looked out over the front of the house. Cat went to the chair and sank onto it. Then she asked, "What did you say to her?"

"The same thing I said to you that day a couple of weeks ago. That what she and I had had was over for me. That it had *been* over for sixteen years."

"That's all?"

"I also told her how I felt about you. That I'm attracted to you, that I want to get close to you, but you won't give me a chance."

"How did Adora react?"

"She listened. And she nodded. But I don't know if she really got the message." He held out his hands, palms up. "What the hell more could I do?"

Cat shook her head, thinking of her sister, of all the things that neither of them had said during their phone conversation a few hours before. A long talk was definitely in order between herself and Adora. She glanced at the window, beyond which the storm still raged.

"Cat." Dillon's voice was soft. "Why is it so important where I talked to Adora, and when?"

She turned from the window to face him once more, thinking there was no reason she had to confess to him how she'd behaved last night. He'd seen her make an idiot of herself with Spike; that was bad enough. He certainly didn't need to hear the rest of it.

But then he came to her and knelt by her knees. She watched him wince when he did it, and an aching tenderness toward him welled up from the deepest part of her to threaten her fragile emotional equilibrium.

"What? What is it?" His face was in shadow, since the lantern was behind him, but his voice was so gentle, so full of honest concern.

For some reason, there seemed nothing else to do but tell him the truth. "I . . . I saw your truck at Adora's last night."

"You what?"

She lifted her hands, then dropped them again in her lap, a gesture as ineffectual as she felt right then. "I couldn't sleep. In the middle of the night, I got up and got dressed and drove to your house. When I got there, I sat in my pickup, wondering what I was doing, wondering if you were inside and if you were...alone. After a while, when sitting there started to make me crazy, I got out of the pickup and marched up to your door and pounded on it for a while."

"Cat." He said her name so gently, and took one of her hands in his.

That gave her the courage to tell the rest, about driving into town, and seeing his Land Cruiser at Adora's.

When she'd told it all, he asked, "If you were wondering what I was doing there, why didn't you just come in and find out?"

She looked down at their joined hands. His were much better groomed than hers, the nails trimmed straight and neat. Her hands looked like what they were: the hands of a carpenter, of a woman of all work.

"Cat?"

She dragged in a breath. "I guess I didn't come in because I didn't really want to know for sure what was happening between you and Adora. Just as you said, what I really wanted was a good excuse to stay away from you."

"Is that still what you want?"

The words *no* and *yes* seemed to take shape in her mind simultaneously. She said neither of them, only looked at his handsome face that was somehow becoming so dear to her, thinking how much she wanted him—and how utterly terrified she was of her own feelings.

Dillon put his hand on her knee to help him rise. Then, when he was standing, he reached down and pulled her to her feet. "I asked you a question. Is that still what you want?"

He was too close. She could hardly think. "Oh, Dillon."

He wrapped an arm around her and brought her closer to him, so that their bodies touched down the front in one long, warm caress. His hand, at the hollow of her back, was firm and sure.

"I love the way you feel," he said. "So strong. And yet there's this softness that you try so hard to hide."

"Dillon . . ."

"Since you walked out on me, it's been a damn seesaw. One minute I'm swearing to get you off my mind. And then the next, I'm dreaming."

"About what?"

"About you. About us. About what it might be like."

"It?"

"It. You and me. Together. Making love."

Her face felt hot and her heart beat faster, to hear him say it out loud that way. Then she thought of the way he'd acted toward her earlier in the day. "But, Dillon, you were so cold today, in the hardware store."

"Damn it, Cat. What the hell did you expect? You tell me to stay out of your life. You don't even say thank you when I rescue you from Spike. And then there you are in the hardware store, looking all worried that I might get lost in the storm. It got to me. I was fed up."

"I know, but . . ."

"Shh. Look. Just kiss me. One time. For now."

Outside, the wind soared up into a long, high moan.

"I don't—"

"Shh. Don't say *don't*."

She was so terribly tempted. "Just one kiss?"

"Just one," he promised with great solemnity. Then a rueful smile lifted the corner of his mouth, changing the shape of the tiny scar on his upper lip. "One for now, anyway. I swear."

"I don't think . . ."

He lifted her chin with the hand that wasn't around her waist. "Yeah. Exactly. Don't think."

"Oh, Dillon."

"Say yes. Say I can kiss you."

"But Dillon . . ."

"I want to hear you say it. It's a simple word. *Yes.*"

"I—"

"Come on."

"Um, I—"

"You can do it."

"Well, I know that."

"Does that mean—?"

"Oh, Dillon."

"Just say it."

"All right. Yes."

Eight

Dillon's lips met hers.

They shared the same breath. It was a gentle, aching, sweet caress. A counterpoint to the wildness of the storm outside.

The hand that had held her chin trailed down her back and joined the other at her waist. He pulled her closer, so that she felt his manhood against her belly, aroused already, promising what might be.

Dillon made a low sound deep in his throat. He teased the shape of her lips with his tongue.

With a sharp little cry of excitement, Cat allowed her lips to part. Her entire body felt so utterly alive. Her breasts brushed his hard chest, and her nipples felt so sensitive against the cotton cups of her bra.

As they had that other time he'd kissed her, her knees seemed to be giving out on her. But this time, Cat didn't care. She twined her arms around Dillon's neck and surrendered to the wonder of the kiss. Her body seemed to be humming; all her nerve endings tingled and yearned.

And then she heard it, at the same time as he did: an angry, bewildered cry.

With a rueful sigh, he grasped her waist and held her just a little away from him. "Do you hear what I hear?"

She nodded. "The baby's awake."

The baby required changing again.

"At this rate," Cat remarked, "we're going to run out of diapers by about midday tomorrow. More than likely, we'll have to improvise with rags. I just hope I've got some old safety pins around here somewhere."

"You'll think of something." Dillon sounded much more complacent about her mothering abilities than Cat felt. He'd found one of the baby's toys—a set of big plastic keys—which he was dangling over the little girl's head as Cat changed the diaper. The baby cooed and gurgled with delight.

Cat went on, "And the formula's all gone. We'll have to try thinned milk and maybe some mashed-up fruit when she gets hungry again. Looks ominous."

Dillon glanced up from his play with the child. "Why's that?"

"Babies' systems are so sensitive. We're in for some digestive upsets, no matter what. And that won't be fun for any of us, believe me."

"Like I said before, you'll work it out."

"I hope so. I wish I knew how old she is. Three or four months, I'd guess. I wonder if she's eating solid food yet at all. It's just been so long since I cared for a baby."

Dillon made an absolutely silly little gurgly sound, to which the baby actually seemed to reply. He lowered the keys enough that her tiny fingers touched them and made them rattle. Then he told Cat, "Don't sweat it. Come on. You'll do your best. What more can you do?"

Cat knew he was right. She told herself to stop worrying as she pressed the tabs in place on the clean diaper.

Then, since the baby seemed so happy, her little fists clenching in awkward grabs for the keys, Cat stretched out beside her on the bed and watched the play between the man and the child. It was a lovely moment, really, with the storm raging outside, and the three of them all cozy and safe together.

In the soft light from the lantern, the baby's skin looked luminous, poreless and perfect. Cat couldn't resist touching her.

Gently Cat laid a hand on the baby's head. She stroked the fine, dark hair and beneath her palm felt the soft depression of the fontanel. The child made a happy, giggly sound, whether in response to Cat's caress or in enjoyment of Dillon's teasing, it was hard to say.

"She could have done worse," Dillon said quietly, "than to have ended up here with us until this storm is through."

Cat shivered at the thought of some of the places a defenseless child might have *ended up*. She looked at Dillon, who seemed to sense her glance and met her eyes.

"I'll get the cradle," she said.

"Good idea."

Cat went upstairs again and came down with a stack of soft cotton rags, two tattered lap quilts and the cradle.

In the kitchen, she wiped the cradle with a soapy cloth, then rinsed it and patted it dry. Then she took one of the quilts and set it inside for a mattress. All this accomplished, she carried the cradle into the bedroom where Dillon was still playing with the baby on the bed.

Dillon looked up from a game of peekaboo as she knelt to set the cradle on the floor. "Looks good," he remarked.

"Hey. Resourceful is my middle name."

The baby reached out and snared Dillon's upper lip. He gummed her fingers and she chortled in delight. Then he took the baby's tiny hand in his and looked at Cat. "And here I thought your middle name was Desiree."

Cat winced at the sound of that name. It had always been a source of embarrassment to her. Her mother had chosen it from an old movie about a mistress of Napoleon. Cat thought it very unsuitable for a down-to-earth person such as herself. She did her best to keep it a secret.

"Ah-ha." Dillon's voice was softly teasing. "I can see it in your face. You *are* sensitive about that name."

She straightened from the cradle. "Who told you?"

"Adora." He watched, bemused, as tiny fingers wrapped themselves around his thumb. "Back in high school. I said I was afraid someday you were actually going to use your daddy's shotgun on me." He grinned at Cat. "And Adora said, 'Cat wouldn't dare. I've told her what will happen if she ever hurts you.'"

His humor was infectious. Cat found herself smiling back at him. "I don't remember this. What had she threatened me with?"

"Telling everyone in town that your middle name is Desiree. Adora said you really despised that name."

Cat groaned a little, thinking back. "I remember now."

"Is that why you never shot me? Because you couldn't stand the embarrassment if your middle name got out?"

Cat pretended to consider this before she answered, "Could be." Then she approached the bed and scooped

up the baby. "Come here, you. Let's check this out."
Carefully she laid the child down in the cradle.

"Not bad," Dillon decided when the child lay on the
old quilt gurgling merrily at the sight of her own feet.
"But in another month or two, it'll be a tight fit."

Cat looked up from the baby to where Dillon still lay
stretched out on the bed. "If we're not out of here in a
month or two, we'll have a lot more problems than a cradle that's too small."

"Amen to that," Dillon agreed as he rolled off the bed
and joined Cat beside the cradle. He took the other lap
quilt and knelt, rather painfully as usual, to tuck it in
around the child.

"Goo-oo-ga," the baby said.

"I think she's comfortable," Dillon decided.

"I think you're right."

They looked up simultaneously and smiled into each
other's eyes.

And it came to Cat that this was the most fun she'd ever
had in a blizzard. In fact, it was the most fun she'd had in
a long time. Her life just plain hadn't centered around
fun.

And then she couldn't help thinking: Could this be *fun*
then, if it became long-term? A man and a baby. A family to care for?

The very things she'd always told herself she *didn't*
want. The things that would tie her down, that would steal
her freedom away just as it had been stolen before she really owned it, when she was only eighteen years old.

But what *was* her freedom, really? Lately, since Dillon
McKenna came back to Red Dog City, her freedom just
hadn't been the same. It had taken on a different meaning. It had begun to seem like nothing more than another
name for loneliness.

"Cat." Her pulse quickened at the tender way he said her name. "What is it? What's on your mind?"

She looked away, toward the door to the kitchen, then made herself look back at the man on the other side of the cradle.

She asked the question she'd been longing to ask for nearly two weeks now. "Would you . . . tell me about Natalie Evans?"

His smile lit up the shadowed room. "Anything. Whatever you want to know."

"I . . ."

But then he reached across the cradle, touched her hand and pointed to the baby. Cat glanced down. The dark lashes lay like tiny fans against the round cheeks. The rosebud mouth made little sucking movements.

Cat looked up at Dillon again. He gestured that they should move into the other room.

"Natalie and I lived together for two years," Dillon said when they were seated at either end of the couch. "We talked about getting married, but somehow that never seemed to happen. I wanted to start a family."

"And she didn't want that?"

"No way. She wasn't about to get herself tied down with any babies. Natalie likes bright lights and good times."

"That's why you broke up, then—because you wanted children and she didn't?"

"Partly, I guess, now I look back. But there was something more immediate that really did the job."

"What?"

"After the accident at the Mirage, it looked for a while as if I might not walk again."

"And?"

"Let's just say she couldn't handle it."

"She broke up with you then?"

"No. Nothing that honest."

"I don't understand."

"You wouldn't." He stretched an arm along the back of the couch to touch her cheek. "That was a compliment."

His hand felt so warm and good. She clasped it in hers. "Thank you. Go on."

"Natalie turned to L.W."

Cat pictured the portly promoter. "L. W. Creedy? She started going out with *him?* But he's sixty, if he's a day."

Dillon chuckled. "Don't underestimate good old L.W. He likes to party hearty. He has plenty of money. And he can *walk.* Which was more than you could have said about me at the time."

"How did you find out?"

"A friend told me. He saw the two of them together, looking *very* cozy, at a club in Century City. It wasn't really a surprise, I have to tell you. I knew by then that Natalie and I weren't making it. I confronted her with what my friend had said about seeing her with L.W. She broke down and cried and said how awful she felt. Don't ask me how it happened, but somehow I ended up comforting *her.* When she settled down, we agreed that it was over between us anyway."

Cat felt a twinge of skepticism. "You certainly took it well."

He shrugged. "By then, there wasn't much to get excited about. As I said, I'd already realized it was over and done. The rough part for me was already past."

"When was the rough part?"

"Right after the accident, the first time she came to see me in the hospital. I'd been in the operating room for twelve hours. I was pretty out of it, but I heard her talking to L.W. before she realized I was awake. The disgust in her voice told me everything. She's not a woman who can take weakness in a man. I knew then that it was all over but the formal goodbyes. So by the time I found out about L.W., I'd had a while to get used to the idea that Natalie and I were through."

"But then why did she show up at your house two weeks ago? Did she want to try again?"

Dillon scoffed. "In a way, I guess you could say that."

"In a way?"

"L.W. sent her."

"He *what?*"

"She was sort of an offering, if you know what I mean. She was supposed to cozy up to me and then talk me into changing my mind about jumping that ravine up near Mount Shasta." Dillon chuckled. "Your face says it all. You're shocked."

"Well, but if she's his *girlfriend,* why would he do a thing like that? I mean, was she supposed to actually—" Cat had to swallow before she could say the word "—*seduce* you?"

"I think that was the general idea."

"*That's* why you were so angry when I told you she was there."

"Uh-huh. I knew right away what L.W. was up to. And I didn't like it one damn bit. But more important than L.W. and Natalie and their scheming little minds, I was thinking about you. Seeing Natalie freaked you out so bad that you turned and ran."

"Yes," she admitted. "It really bothered me. She came out of nowhere. And she was so beautiful. And I guess I was..."

"Jealous?" He provided the word for her.

She squeezed his hand and confessed, "Yeah. And confused. But you haven't told me what happened—when you went upstairs to see her?"

"Nothing much. I told her flat out that I wasn't falling for L.W.'s little scheme."

Cat couldn't resist asking, "Did you *cook* her anything?"

Dillon looked offended. "Hell, no. I got rid of her, pronto."

"Good."

He slanted her a glance. "Why?"

"She didn't deserve to eat your cooking."

He lowered his eyes. She could see he was pleased. "All I had on my mind then was how I'd explain everything to you when you came back the next day."

Cat felt contrite. "But I didn't *let* you explain."

Now he was looking right at her. "It's a failing of yours."

She spoke evenly. "I know. I'm working on it."

"Good. Any more questions?"

She thought about that, then told him, "No. Not for now."

He nodded. "Okay, then."

For a time, they sat there, holding hands, saying nothing. Cat enjoyed the shared silence. For the first time since the day Natalie Evans had appeared at Dillon's house, they were comfortable with each other. Outside, the storm continued unabated.

A little later, Cat showed him to one of the two rooms upstairs. She pointed out where the extra blankets were stored, feeling a little constrained, a little awkward about this whole business of where he would sleep.

But he didn't seem to be pushing for anything—and she wasn't about to throw herself into his arms. So she showed him the bed and the blankets and then she led him to the one bathroom, which was off the kitchen, next to her own bedroom.

"If you want a shower, take it now," she advised. "The hot water heater's electric. If the power stays out, we're going to be taking sponge baths after tonight."

"A shower sounds great. And I'll make it quick, so you can have one, too."

While Dillon took his turn in the bathroom, Cat managed to slide the cradle, with the sleeping baby in it, into the kitchen. It would be warmer there deep in the night as the fires dwindled to embers and the cold outside seeped in.

Cat took her shower when Dillon was done and then climbed into bed.

But she wasn't there for long. Less than an hour later, Cat was pushing the covers back and sliding her bare feet into her moccasins, which waited on the floor. She had heard the little whimpers starting up. Once her moccasins were on, she paused on the edge of the bed, unmoving, for a moment or two, just in case the baby might lapse back into slumber.

No such luck. The whimpers grew louder, and were interspersed with little groans and yelps.

Cat lit the lamp in the bedroom, then hurried to the other room. "Okay, okay. I'm here. Settle down now."

She took another moment to light the lamp, then scooped up the squirming child and carried her to the bedroom, where she changed her diaper. That produced a moment of quiet.

But then the little girl started crying again. Cat knew what the problem was. Hunger.

She put the baby on her shoulder and patted her back. "All right, now. I understand. We'll figure out something. You come on with me."

She started for the kitchen again—and there was Dillon standing in the doorway to the living room, wearing his jeans and his socks and a sleepy grin.

"You look adorable in a union suit," he said. She hardly had time to blush when he added, "What's the problem?"

She reminded herself to pay attention to the baby, not Dillon's furred chest and muscular arms. "She's hungry, I think."

"What'll we do about it?"

Cat gently jiggled the fussing baby as she tried to decide. "Let's try some mashed banana for starters, and then we'll dilute some milk in warm water and give that to her to drink."

"Good enough."

Dillon went right to work mashing up the banana. Then he held the baby on his lap as Cat spooned the fruit into the tiny mouth. It seemed to go down well enough.

After that, they put the thinned, warm milk into a bottle. The baby made a face at the taste. But after a few minutes, she was sucking away. As Dillon held her and fed her the bottle, Cat built up both of the fires and put big pots of water on them so that later they'd have hot water for washing and whatever else they might need it for.

At last, an hour and a half after she'd awakened, the baby fell asleep again. Dillon handed her to Cat, who laid her in the cradle once more and covered her with the quilt.

When the baby was tucked in to Cat's satisfaction, Cat looked up at Dillon to whisper something innocuous about how things should be quiet for a while now.

But the words—whatever they might have been—died in her throat.

Dillon was watching her. The look on his face stole the breath from her lungs.

Nine

Slowly Cat rose to her feet. "Dillon, I..."

He put his hand to his lips and whispered, "You'll wake her." Then he bent and blew out the lamp that glowed beside them on the kitchen table.

The kitchen receded into shadow. There was the popping of the fire in the stove and the soft, even breathing of the child. Outside, the storm seemed to have quieted. The turbulence now was right here in this small room, an intimate turbulence—between Cat and the man on the other side of the cradle.

Cat couldn't look away. The light from the lamp in the bedroom behind her showed her his face. There was such intensity there. Such promise. And such pure determination.

Hardly realizing she did it, Cat began to back up, away from the cradle and into her bedroom.

Dillon followed, matching her every step with one of his own, edging around the sleeping baby and into her private space. When he was through the doorway, he reached out, his eyes still locked with hers, and pushed the door shut behind him.

Cat felt the backs of her shaking knees meet the end of the bed. "It'll get cold in here, if you shut that door." Her voice sounded so husky, she hardly recognized it as her own.

Dillon ignored her remark. He got right to the point. "Come here, Cat."

"I...um..."

"Cat."

She had that weak feeling again, as if her legs might give out on her.

"Cat."

"All right." Her voice was still husky and alien. The air in the room seemed thicker, somehow. "I'm coming."

He smiled then, a slow, knowing smile.

She took a step toward him. Then another. Then one more. Now she was within touching distance.

But he didn't touch her. He carefully kept his hands at his sides. "I was going to wait. I don't know what for. It seemed like the right thing to do. To give you more time. But there was something about you. Tucking that baby in, crouched over that crib in your long underwear. I don't want to wait for you anymore, Cat."

Cat looked at him, at all of him—at his handsome face, his dark eyes and the lightning-bolt scar on his lip. At the cleft in his chin and the strong column of his neck. At his wide, muscled shoulders. There was a scar on his left shoulder that followed the shape of the joint and disappeared beneath his arm. It was very white against his bronze skin. In fact, now that she looked closer, there were scars everywhere. Beneath its mat of dark hair, his broad, hard chest was peppered with them.

"Cat? What do you say?"

"I...um..."

His mouth curved upward again. "You already said that."

She made herself think of something more pertinent. "I...don't really know how." And then she groaned a little. "*I don't know how*. Is that a dumb remark, or what?"

He shook his head. "Not dumb. Not dumb at all. You've never made love before, is that what you're saying?"

She was nodding before he even finished. "Right. No. I never have."

"Hey. It's okay." But he was looking rueful.

Her skin felt hot. She knew she was blushing. Around him, she blushed all the time. "What? What is it?"

"Nothing. I just...it occurred to me that I've hardly come here prepared."

"Prepared for what?"

"To make love with you."

Awareness dawned. "Oh. You mean—"

"Right, protection against pregnancy. I haven't got anything."

"Oh."

He gave a low laugh at the absurdity of the situation. "Can you believe this? Finally, the moment I've been dreaming of. And I'm unprepared."

"It's okay." There was a lump in her throat. She coughed to clear it. "Wait right here."

He looked at her sideways. "Don't worry, I'm not going anywhere." She felt his gaze on her back as she marched across the room and pulled out a bureau drawer.

Cat reached in and found the box containing twelve condoms that she'd stuck in there a few months ago. She pulled out the box, shoved the drawer shut and then marched right back to Dillon. "Here."

He stared down at her outstretched hand, then up into her face, which she just knew was the color of a ripe tomato. "Well," he said. "Thanks." He took the box.

She felt defensive and that sharpened her tongue. "Don't look so stunned. Just because I've never done this before doesn't mean I haven't planned ahead. More or less."

He lifted a dark brow. "More or less?"

She backed up enough to drop onto the end of the bed. "Oh, all right. Adora gave them to me a few months ago. So I could be *safe* and *smart* if the impossible ever happened." Now she felt mortified. She couldn't look at him.

He approached and stood over her. She stared down at his stocking feet.

"Cat."

"What?"

He tossed the box on the bed behind her and then turned and sat at her side. She felt the bed give at his weight, tipping her body a little closer to him.

"Cat." His voice was soft. An invitation and a caress.

She warmed to it, yet still resisted just a little, clinging to the last shreds of her defensiveness. She folded her hands together, stuck them between her knees and hunched her shoulders.

He put his arm around her, and pulled her close. The minute their bodies touched, she relaxed.

"That's better." He kissed her temple, a light, quick brush of his lips. Then gently, he guided her head to rest against him.

He was warm, his chest hard. The mat of hair there was crisp and wiry as it rubbed her cheek.

For a little while, he simply held her that way, stroking her hair and rubbing her shoulder. She remembered again how much she liked the smell of him and the feeling of support and safety she felt in his arms.

But then, soon enough, he was guiding her back. She kicked off her moccasins as he urged her to lie down full-length on the bed, helping her to scoot up, so that her head was on the pillows. The box she'd given him was in the way, so he took it and put it on the night table. And then he lay on his side next to her.

He kissed her, a long, drugging kiss. And as he kissed her, he touched her neck, stroking it as if to soothe her. His hand strayed, to caress the shape of her ear. And then his fingers moved lower, to the row of buttons that ran down the front of her long johns from the hollow of her neck to the juncture of her thighs.

With slow, deliberate care, he unbuttoned those buttons, starting with the top one, placing a sweet, arousing kiss on each new bit of skin that was revealed as the buttons gave way.

When the buttons were all undone, he reached in the long opening. She gasped at the feel of his hand on her breast. And then she sighed as he toyed with her, rubbing each of her nipples in turn.

Very gently, he peeled back the long johns. Cat closed her eyes. He lowered his head. Cat gasped. His mouth was on her breast. He stroked it maddeningly with his tongue. Then, leaving little, nipping kisses in a trail across her chest, his mouth found her other breast.

His hand kept roaming as he suckled her breasts. Cat found she couldn't lie still. She wriggled and moaned out hungry, encouraging noises, noises that shocked her a little, they sounded so wild and abandoned.

She felt his hand skim over her belly and move lower. He combed his fingers through the soft nest of curls at the apex of her thighs.

And then he found the heart of her. She gasped and moaned.

"Ah," he said on a long exhalation. He stroked her there, taking his time.

As he stroked her, he kissed his way, lingeringly, from her breasts, up over her collarbone, to her neck and her chin.

At last, he reached her mouth. "Kiss me, Cat," he said against her lips.

She moaned an affirmative as his mouth closed over hers. His tongue swept beyond her parted lips as his fingers continued their incredible play below.

"I knew it," he whispered. "A woman. All woman. No hiding it here."

His touch urged her on. She had no will, right then, no strength. She was only what he had called her. A woman. A woman, in the eye of a storm, at the hands of a man.

He said very softly, "Come. Come for me...."

And she did. Just as he said it, her body pulsing and releasing, the fulfillment starting at the core of her and spreading like a blinding light to the ends of her fingers, the tips of her toes.

As the intense release faded into afterglow, Cat lay looking up at him through dazed eyes. He smiled at her, an intimate, tender smile. Then he slid off the bed long enough to slip off his jeans and his socks. She blinked when she saw him, naked before her, his manhood rising strong and ready from the dark thatch between his thighs.

But there was more. More than the urgent evidence of his desire. And as she looked at him, a single tear was born at the corner of her eye. She felt it spill over and trail down her cheek.

He knew what made her cry—the long scars on his thighs, like white grooves cut terribly deep in the powerful flesh. One sliced down the front of his left leg, ending in a burst of pearly tissue at the knee. The other furrowed down the outside of his right thigh.

"Pretty ugly, huh? Pretty much of a damn mess." The words were soft, and only a little bitter.

She bit her lip to keep the tears back, furiously shaking her head. "Not ugly," she managed to tell him. "Not ugly at all."

She sat up and slid near him. And, to show him that she meant what she said, she placed a kiss on his left leg, right above the knee, at the deepest part of the white scar there.

"Cat." The word was ripped from him.

He grabbed her shoulders, his fingers digging in. He held her hard at arm's length and looked at her, deep into her eyes.

And then everything happened at once. He yanked at the cloth of her long johns. "Take it off. Get it out of the way."

She nodded, and set to work as he turned and fumbled with the contents of the box on the night table. Swiftly, roughly, she jerked her arms from the sleeves, shoved the long johns down to her waist and slithered out of them. She tossed them on the floor and raised her arms to Dillon just as he slid the condom in place.

"Cat." He came down to her, awkwardly, roughly, moving between her thighs, positioning himself. "I can't . . . I want . . ."

She put her hand on his mouth. "Shh. It's okay. Please. Come here. To me."

He groaned then. And she felt him, there at her entrance. She wrapped her arms around him and pulled him down, crying out as he breached the thin hindrance of her innocence.

In that single thrust, he was all the way in. He held himself there, on a long, hungry groan. "I hurt you...."

"It's okay."

"I didn't mean to hurt you. I wanted to make this—"

"Shh."

She held his head in the crook of her neck and shoulder. She stroked his hair. And she felt him, felt the way he was holding himself, on the brink, trying to keep himself contained.

"Let it happen," she commanded on a whisper. "It's all right. It's just fine."

He groaned again, an agonized sound. And then, at last, he sighed. A sigh of release. And surrender. She felt him then, pulsing inside her as he gave himself up to the soft pressure of her body around him.

When he was done, he rolled away and threw a hand over his face. He moaned.

Cat missed the feel of his body against hers. She turned and pressed herself close to his side. He moved his arm so she could rest her head on his chest.

Idly he stroked her hair. "Talk about a lackluster performance," he muttered at the top of her head.

She lifted up enough to punch his shoulder. "Shut up. We'll do better. It was our first time together. And *my* first time, period."

He wrapped a short curl of her hair around his finger. "It's been a long time for me—since my last time. More than a year." He chuckled dryly. "That's my excuse."

"You don't need an excuse, Dillon. Not with me."

He was quiet for a moment. "I know that. And I'm glad."

She wanted to be sure of what he had said before. "You mean you haven't made love since before the accident in Las Vegas?"

"Yeah."

She rested her head on his chest and ran her fingers through the hair over one of his small, masculine nipples. "Dillon?"

"Um?"

"Even though it was short, I think I could get to like it."

He chuckled then. "Good."

"And I don't think your scars are ugly."

He said nothing for a moment. He'd stopped stroking her hair. "Then why did the sight of them make you cry?" His voice was gruff, torn sounding.

She lifted her head and looked into his eyes. "Several reasons."

"Tell me."

She was quiet for a moment. She wanted to say this just right.

At last, she explained, "I cried because I didn't realize before how close you must have come to never walking again."

"I see."

"And there's more."

"There is?"

"Yes. I also cried because of what it must have been like—the pain and the fear...and the plain hard, grueling work to get on your feet again. All that took so much courage, I think. So much undiluted grit. You just... amazed me, that's all."

The little flecks in his eyes were gleaming. He put his hand on her head and guided it down to his chest again. Then he recommenced stroking her hair. She could hear the steady *thub-dub* of his heart against her ear.

"And I *never* cry, Dillon McKenna," she added in a rough little whisper.

His laugh was good and deep against her ear. "Amen to that, Cat Beaudine."

In a little while, they got up and went to the bathroom, where they took turns giving each other sponge baths with the now-chilly water from the hot water tap. The sponge baths led to more love play.

They ended up back in Cat's bed. Dillon guided her to the top position this time, teasing that he knew it was one she'd enjoy.

And it was. She sank upon him carefully, her inner flesh still tender from this new experience called lovemaking.

But soon enough, she was rocking slow and sweet above him, pausing to seek a new rhythm, then speeding up, then slowing down once more.

They went on like that for a long time. Cat reveled in it. She looked down at Dillon's dark head against her white pillows, at his strong, clean-cut face contorted in ecstasy. And she saved every touch, every smell, every sound. She saved them in her heart, as her body experienced them. Outside was the storm and in the other room a lost child was sleeping. But here, in this room, there was pleasure...never-ending rapture. It went on and on.

At last, Cat felt fulfillment approaching, rolling up from the center of her, expanding out to take over the night. She cried out, her body clutching him. He moaned in response. And then he was pulsing into her, just as her body closed and opened around him.

She fell with a soft sigh against his chest. He wrapped his arms around her and stroked her—long, slow caresses down the center of her back.

Sleep approached. She welcomed it as she did the stroking hand on her bare skin.

The next morning, it was still snowing. The phone lines and electricity remained out. The baby was fussy and seemed uncomfortable, no doubt from the unaccustomed foods she was eating. They took turns holding and rocking her.

At two in the afternoon, they used the last disposable diaper. After that, they turned to the rags Cat had gathered up—and the two precious safety pins she'd found in her mending kit.

By then, Dillon was doing his share of diaper changing. Cat was grateful for small favors, especially when Dillon also pitched right in with laundering the makeshift diapers—a long, unpleasant job that had to be done by hand, using the hot water they boiled on the stove. Also, the improvised diapers didn't fit too tightly. So accidents were always happening. But then, Dillon got clever and invented a sort of diaper cover out of plastic wrap that cut the leaks to a minimum.

Upstairs, they strung a sturdy length of thin rope for a clothesline. They filled it up with an endless succession of "diapers," quilts, and old rags—and, at one point, even Dillon's jeans. The jeans were badly soiled when one of the baby's accidents occurred while Dillon was bouncing her on his lap after he'd taken off a dirty diaper—and before he'd bothered to put on a fresh one. Cat produced an old pair of overalls that had once belonged to her father. Dillon wore them while he waited for his only pair of pants to dry.

The refrigerator became a true icebox. They brought in two bowls of snow and set them on the bottom shelves to keep the compartment cool. The contents of the freezer presented no problem. Cat put all of that out on the side porch in a big plastic storage bin.

Whenever there was a daytime break in the snow and the baby was quiet, they'd get out the shovels and do what they could to try to clear the driveway to the road. But the storm that first night had given the snow a big head start on them. It was slow, hard work. And beneath the new snow, the old layers would freeze in the night. They needed a good half a day without any new snowfall before they would really see progress in digging themselves out.

But their isolation wasn't all hardship. Not by any means.

Cat and Dillon found time to play Scrabble—Cat was the best with thinking up obscure words and finding high-scoring places to put them, but Dillon was the most willing to cheat. After Cat would finally beat him at the Scrabble game, they'd each choose from the books that lined Cat's walls and retire to her bed, where they would lie side by side, reading, sharing a mutual and contented silence by the light of the kerosene lamps.

And between the silences, it seemed to Cat that they talked endlessly, about everything and nothing. The only subject they avoided, by some sort of tacit agreement, was the future.

And as the time passed, the baby seemed to settle in as they did. By the third day, Saturday, she seemed to have adjusted a little to watered-down cow's milk and mashed fruits and vegetables. "Accidents" were less frequent; so were fussing and crying.

The world they'd created with just the three of them in it became an idyllic place, a magic place, without past or future. To Cat, for those days of the storm, it seemed that there was only now. There was taking care of the baby and of each other.

And there was making love.

Though she and Dillon tended the baby and shoveled the driveway, played Scrabble and read and talked all the time, it seemed to Cat that what they did the most was make love.

Dillon loved to make love.

And Cat liked it just fine, too.

She found Dillon could be very inventive. Once they made love in her great-grandmother's rocking chair, with Dillon on the bottom and Cat sitting on his lap. He whispered in her ear that he was rocking her to heaven and she burst into fits of giggles that woke the baby.

So naturally, a few hours later, when the baby was sleeping again, they had to pick up where they'd left off. When it was over, she bit his earlobe and admitted that he'd been right. She'd been all the way to heaven, without leaving that chair.

And then on Saturday, during another of their rather ineffectual sojourns outside to try once more to shovel the driveway, Dillon came up behind her and stuck a handful of snow down the back of her pants. Cat shrieked in outrage, dropped her shovel and grabbed up a handful of snow of her own.

Dillon stood his ground, his eyes glittering devilishly at her. "Don't you dare."

She advanced on him. "*You* dared."

"That was different."

"Wrong." In a flash, she grabbed the front of his jeans and shoved the wad of snow in there. Unfortunately the jeans were snug. Her gloved hand got stuck.

Dillon started laughing. He fell on top of her, chortling away. "Now, I've got you where I want you." He put on a voice like a villain in a bad melodrama.

She wriggled and tried to punch him. "Get off me."

Now he pretended to look hurt. "Say you don't mean that."

"Dillon, it's freezing out here."

"Let me warm you up."

Somehow, she managed to yank her hand out of his jeans. But the glove stuck there. She looked into his eyes and saw what he was thinking. "Oh, no. Not here in the driveway."

Now he waxed poetic—as he fumbled for the zipper of her pants. "The snow will be our bed."

"Why can't the *bed* be our bed? Please?"

"I love it when you beg me." He pulled her glove free of his jeans and tossed it aside. She looked up into his eyes, trying for a glare.

Yet she did nothing to stop him as he took off his own glove with his teeth and his cold hand found its way under her jacket and the layers of her shirt and underwear to close over her breast.

She shivered—and then she sighed.

He chuckled and guided her hand to the placket of his jeans.

The feel of him, against her palm, aroused and ready beneath the cold, wet spot the melting snow had left, made her forget that she was freezing and the snow was starting to come down again, made her forget everything but Dillon.

"Ah, Cat..." he breathed against her mouth.

She smiled and opened her mouth beneath his, tasting him. And they helped each other to part and lower their clothing enough that their bodies could join.

When he pulled a condom from his pocket she tried to glare at him again. "You planned this."

He slid the thing on. "I did. I'm guilty. Punish me."

But all she could do was moan and sigh as he lowered himself upon her once more. He settled her legs around him, and then he came into her.

She groaned as she felt him, filling her.

"Say that again," he murmured in her ear.

And she did, several times. It felt so wonderful, so right, to have him within her. He began to move, and she moved with him, there in the bed of snow on the side of the driveway.

When fulfillment claimed her, she opened her eyes. The sky was a whirl of white. The snowflakes fell on her up-turned face, first dry, then cold and wet, as her body heat melted them. She cried out, clutching Dillon even closer. He thrust hard against her, finding and surrendering to his own satisfaction.

The moment spun out. Cat went with it, riding it, reveling in it. It was a moment of purest beauty, she thought in a shattered sort of way. The moment when the two of them were one in the heart of the storm.

A few minutes later, they got up, put their shovels in the woodshed off the side porch and staggered inside. They found the baby awake, giggling and waving her arms at the ceiling. The power was still out. When Dillon tried the phone, as they did every few hours, he found it as dead as it had been since Thursday afternoon.

They made dinner and ate, then fed the baby. They washed "diapers." When the baby went to sleep, they read for a while, then made love again.

At three the next morning, the baby woke. They rose together and changed and fed her.

"Listen," Dillon whispered when the little girl was slumbering once again in his arms.

"What?"

"It's quiet. Outside." He laid the baby down in the cradle.

They quickly dressed and went out the side door to stand in the driveway, where another six inches of snow had fallen since that afternoon. Above, the stars were like pinpoints of ice, far away in the black of the sky.

"It's cleared off since we went to bed," Cat said. "This may be it."

"What?" His voice was gruff.

"The day we get out."

Roughly he reached for her and pulled her to him.

The sudden movement surprised her. "Dillon?"

He said nothing, only lowered his lips to hers for a kiss so achingly sweet that she felt a great sadness when it came to an end.

"Oh, Dillon..." She reached up and wrapped her arms around his neck.

"What?"

"Do that again."

"Be glad to." He kissed her once more, and then he led her inside, where he made love to her with a fierce, consuming hunger that stunned her and left her, at the last, feeling marked by him, *his* in a way she had never known she could be.

When daylight came, it brought the sun. They had to step outside or go upstairs to see it, because the snow was piled in drifts above the windows on the first floor. As soon as they'd eaten and made the baby comfortable, they went out to try once more to clear the driveway.

The power came on at nine. Cat went in to check on the baby and found that the kitchen light was on. She checked the phone, but it was still out. So she turned on the television in the living room to a Reno station and called to Dillon outside that they had electricity again. He stopped shoveling long enough to wave an acknowledgment at her.

She retreated into the warmth of the house and heated some watered-down milk for the baby.

Then she took the child and the bottle to the living room and got comfortable in the big easy chair.

The baby was half finished with her bottle when the news flash came on.

"Little Alexa Todd is still missing today," the announcer said as a snapshot of a very young baby in a frilly lavender dress filled the screen. "The Reno baby disappeared almost seventy-two hours ago, when a mentally disturbed woman abducted her from a local market and allegedly left her in the rear section of a large red four-by-four vehicle. Authorities are hoping that now that the big storm is clearing, the owner of the vehicle will come forward with information leading to the safe recovery of the four-month-old girl."

The picture of the baby disappeared and was replaced by a shot of pine trees and snow and what appeared to be a buried highway. "In other major news, the three-day blizzard is over at last, leaving much of Northern California still trying to dig itself out after what many are calling the worst storm in two decades...."

The voice droned on, but Cat hardly heard it. She was still thinking of the snapshot she'd seen seconds ago. The baby in the picture had been even younger than the one

Cat held in her arms. But Cat would have known those eyes anywhere, and that little dimpled chin.

Their lost baby had a name—and parents who were probably suffering the agonies of the damned right about now. The thought of what it must be like for them mobilized Cat.

She stood, jiggling the baby enough that her little mouth came off the bottle with a hollow popping sound. The baby looked up, wide-eyed, at Cat.

"It's all right, honey. Don't worry." Cat crooned. "We'll get you to your mommy and daddy now, just as soon as we can."

Cat went to the phone and put the receiver to her ear. It was still dead.

Pausing only to lay the baby safely in the cradle, she went to tell Dillon that they had to get into town fast.

Ten

It took them three more hours of backbreaking effort, but by noon, they had shoveled the driveway clear enough to get the Land Cruiser out to the road. They went back inside then, where they found that the phone still wasn't working.

So they took a few minutes to clean up a little and bolt down a hasty lunch.

After that, Cat fed and changed the baby, snapping her into a clean blanket sleeper and wrapping her in her pink blanket with one of the quilts over that for extra warmth. Then, with the baby in her arms, Cat hooked the diaper bag over her shoulder and followed Dillon out the door.

In the driveway, they met up with Nestor Brinkman, who worked for the county and who'd been two years ahead of Cat in school. Nestor was behind the wheel of the county snowplow. He'd decided to give Cat a hand,

and widened the path she and Dillon had already cut in the snow.

Cat thanked him.

"No problem." Nestor exchanged greetings with Dillon, but his eyes were on the bundle in Cat's arms. "What's that you got there?"

"A baby."

"A *what?*" Nestor grinned. "You're a pair of quick operators, all right."

Cat gave him a patient look. "Very funny, Nestor."

Dillon explained briefly how he'd found the baby in his truck and that they were pretty sure it was the infant that had disappeared in Reno a few days ago.

Nestor could hardly believe it. "Hey, I heard of that baby. It's been all over the news."

Cat nodded. "The phone lines are still out, so we can't call anyone and tell them. We need to get her in to the sheriff's station right away."

"Good thinkin'," Nestor declared. "Listen, you'll find the road clear all the way through to town. And I got my radio here. I'll call ahead and tell 'em you're on the way." He was already on the radio as he backed the plow down the driveway.

The trip was slow; the roads were clear but dangerously icy. The baby, lulled by the motion of the truck, fell asleep right away. Dillon kept his eyes on the treacherous highway ahead of them.

Cat stared straight ahead, too, as if she could will the truck to move faster; it seemed so urgent that they reach town as soon as possible.

But it was so quiet in the truck, with the baby sleeping and Dillon concentrating on getting them there without mishap. After a while, Cat's mind began to wander. She began to ponder things that might have been better left alone. She began to realize that urgency wasn't the only thing she felt. Beneath all the rush to do what had to be done, lay sadness and an awful sense of impending loss.

For an enchanted three days, she and Dillon had played house with this child from nowhere. Yet very shortly, the baby who now slept so trustingly in Cat's arms would be back with her real parents where she belonged. Cat might never see those wide blue eyes again.

Gently Cat adjusted the blanket around the tiny, sleeping face. She knew she should feel good—proud, even. Cat and Dillon had done their absolute best for the little one, who would go back to her mother and father healthy and happy. What might have been a tragedy would become one of those stories her parents would tell her as she grew up, how she was lost in a blizzard and cared for by kind strangers for three whole days.

Kind strangers.

That's what Dillon and Cat would be to her. That's what Dillon and Cat *were* to her, really. There was nothing to be gained from denying the truth.

It was just that at some point, during those magical three days of the storm, Cat had slipped over the line and started to think of this baby as hers.

Just as she had let herself think of Dillon as hers.

"Cat?"

She looked up to meet Dillon's worried glance.

"Cat, are you okay?"

"Fine. Yes, I'm fine."

When they reached the sheriff's station, they saw right away that Nestor's message had gotten through. Wanda Spooner, who was Lizzie's sister-in-law and also the local representative for Child Protective Services, was already there.

Two deputies stood flanking Wanda when Dillon and Cat walked through the glass doors into the reception area. One of the deputies was Don Peebles, a local man. The other was someone Cat didn't know.

"Well," Don said, "you folks are a sight for sore eyes, I gotta say." Introductions were quickly accomplished and then Don and the other deputy led Dillon off to take his statement about how he'd found the baby.

Wanda and Cat were left staring at each other over the bundle of blankets in which the child was now beginning to stir.

"Here, I'll take her." Wanda held out her hands.

Cat passed the baby over. Neither she nor Wanda was too careful of the quilt. During the switch, it slipped toward the tiled floor.

"That's all right. You hold on to that," Wanda suggested.

Cat straightened with the quilt. Right then, the baby started making urgent little whimpering noises. Her tiny hands reached out, as if she begged to be taken back.

"There, there. It's okay," Wanda soothed.

Cat clutched the quilt close and looked away. She had a wild and impossible urge right then to snatch the child out of Wanda's arms and run back out the glass doors.

Wanda went on talking softly to the baby. Cat dared to look again. The baby was quiet, staring solemnly at Wanda.

Wanda adjusted the pink blanket more comfortably around her. "Yes. It's all right. It's just fine." Wanda looked up at Cat. "Her parents have been notified. They're on the way."

"Good. That's good," Cat heard herself saying. But her arms were aching with emptiness.

Wanda went on whispering to the baby. Cat looked away again, longing to be out of there. She stared beyond the reception counter, toward the place where Dillon had disappeared with the two deputies, presumably into a back room somewhere. She wished he would hurry.

"I suppose I should take the diaper bag," Wanda said.

"What?" Cat made herself look at Wanda and the little pink bundle in her arms once more.

"The diaper bag?"

"Oh, yes. Of course." Cat slipped it off her arm and handed it over. Then she remembered what Wanda was going to find when she looked inside. "We ran out of diapers on Friday, so there are only rags in there, I'm afraid. We've been using them as diapers. And plastic wrap for plastic pants."

Wanda smiled. "You were resourceful."

Resourceful. The word echoed in her head.

Resourceful is my middle name, she'd said.

And Dillon had replied, *And here I thought your middle name was Desiree....*

It had been the most fun she'd ever had in a blizzard.

The most fun she'd had, period. In her whole life. Herself and Dillon and the little lost baby. An instant family. For three wonderful days.

And now it was over. The real world was closing in.

Behind Cat, the glass doors swung open. A blast of cold air swirled around the room and was cut off as the doors closed again. The county sheriff had arrived, with two other deputies.

The sheriff strode right up to her. "Catherine Beaudine?"

"Yes." Overhead, the fluorescent lights seemed glaringly bright. Somewhere in back, where they'd taken Dillon, rock 'n' roll music played. From a big two-way radio beyond the counter, there was the constant drone of voices and static.

The sheriff grabbed her hand and pumped it enthusiastically. "This is wonderful news. Terrific." He looked at Wanda Spooner. "How is she?" He glanced at the baby in Wanda's arms.

"She looks just fine, Sheriff."

"Good, good." He put his arm around Cat and gave her a broad smile. "As soon as you're finished with Wanda here, we want a full report of all that happened."

Cat tried to smile back at him. She could see he was well-meaning, but all she could think about at that moment was that she wanted him to take his heavy hand off her shoulder. "I'd be glad to tell you anything you need to know."

"Good, good." The sheriff squeezed her shoulder and then let go.

Wanda asked, "What has she been eating?"

Cat's mind seemed to be operating in slow motion. "Excuse me?"

"The baby. What have you been feeding her?"

Cat told her.

"Digestive problems?"

"Yes, at first. But she seems to have adjusted pretty well."

"Great. Anything else I should know?" Cat must have looked at her blankly because Wanda hastened to elaborate. "About Alexa. Any rashes, strange reactions—has she run a temperature?"

"Not that I noticed."

The glass doors opened again. Xavier Mott, one of Red Dog City's two family practice physicians, came in. "Here's the doctor now." Wanda looked down at the baby and spoke with teasing gentleness. "He'll check you out good." Then she turned to the sheriff. "Okay, you can have Cat now. If I need to ask more questions, I'll catch her before she leaves."

"Good, good," the sheriff told Wanda. He led Cat behind the long counter, into a hallway with rooms branching off of it. He chose a room and took her in there. She sat in a chair in front of a desk, where another deputy, a woman, waited at a computer screen. The deputy asked for her full name, address and phone number. Dutifully Cat gave the deputy the information, which the deputy entered into the computer.

"Okay." The sheriff gave Cat his wide, politician's smile. "Would you just tell us how you found the baby and everything that's happened since then?"

It was a big order. Cat told him what he needed to know, explaining how they'd brought the baby right to the station at the very first opportunity, as soon as they could get a vehicle out of her driveway. The sheriff listened to most of the story without comment, only stopping her to ask a few questions right at first when she explained what Dillon had told her about how the baby came to be in his Land Cruiser. She was just finishing up when Dillon appeared with the two deputies, Don Peebles and the one Cat didn't know, who had been at the station when they arrived.

"What do you think, Don?" the sheriff asked.

Don Peebles shrugged. "What I got from Dillon here fits the story we have from the Rankin woman. She claims she left the baby in a red four-by-four in the same station where it turns out Dillon stopped for gas. He left his truck to go to the rest room, and she put the baby in the back."

Dillon asked, "But why?"

The sheriff hitched a leg up on the desk and shook his head. "Sad story. The Rankin woman's own baby died about three months ago of pneumonia. The child was a girl. About the same age as the Todd child. Evidently the Rankin woman has been unstable since her baby's death. She saw little Alexa in a stroller in the market. And when Alexa's mother's back was turned—"

"She *stole* the baby." Dillon finished the sentence for him.

"Right," the other deputy said. "But then she got scared. She was confused, not thinking straight. When the Reno police questioned her, she claimed she'd tucked the baby in, all nice and cozy, in the back of a big, warm four-by-four."

"But it all worked out, thanks to you folks," the sheriff added.

"We're glad we could help."

All Cat could think was that the moment of escape was near at last. "Are you finished with us, then?"

There was another flurry of thanks and appreciation, and the sheriff agreed that of course they could go.

Dillon nodded. "Give us a call if there's anything else."

"We will."

Cat stood. Dillon held out his hand and Cat took it, glad for the firmness of his grip and the reassuring warmth of his touch. However, she could have sworn she heard Don Peebles, whom she'd known since kindergarten, suck in a little gasp of surprise behind her. No doubt he couldn't believe what he was seeing: Cat Beaudine holding hands with a *man*.

The other deputy cleared his throat. "This way, folks."

He escorted them out to the reception area again, but then asked them to wait when the deputy behind the desk signaled to him. The two conferred briefly, then the deputy who'd led them out of the back area turned to Cat and Dillon.

"Wanda wants to see you before you go." He indicated the row of chairs that waited along the wall on either side of the double doors. "Have a seat."

Ignoring the deputy's advice, Cat and Dillon remained standing while Wanda was summoned. As the minutes ticked by, Cat felt more and more uncomfortable. It was such a public place. And anyone who passed by could see that she and Dillon were holding hands. She tugged a little, hoping he'd just release her and let it go at that.

Instead he winked at her, leaned in close and whispered in her ear, "Not a chance."

Cat cut her eyes away, feeling her face turn crimson.

That was when she saw the woman staring at her.

The woman was pretty and young, dressed in a red coat, with a red mohair tam on her strawberry-colored hair. She sat in one of the chairs by the door, wearing an expression of stark disbelief. Cat knew what she was thinking: The woman could not comprehend what a man like Dillon could see in a person like Cat.

Right then, Wanda appeared. "Thanks for waiting."

All Cat could think of was that Wanda didn't have the child with her. "Where's the baby?" she demanded.

"Don't worry," Wanda soothed. "Alexa's fine. Doc Mott is giving her a checkup."

"Oh. All right, then," Cat said, and felt foolish and pushy. She tried to be more civil. "You wanted to talk to us again?"

"Yes. I was hoping you'd wait until the Todds arrive. They should be here in a half hour at the most."

Cat stared at Wanda. Staying to meet the baby's parents was the last thing she wanted to do.

Dillon seemed to sense Cat's distress. He asked diplomatically, "Is there some reason they need to meet with us?"

"No reason other than to say thank you, really." Wanda's voice was gentle. "To meet the people who took such good care of their child."

Dillon looked at Cat. "Well, what do you think?"

Cat gave a tiny, tight shake of her head. She just couldn't do it. Not right now. It was all too much, all the noise and bustle and glaring lights; Dillon holding her hand and Don Peebles gasping at the sight; the pretty woman ogling her in disbelief. She felt as if she'd awakened to a nightmare after the quiet and wonder of the past three days.

Dillon answered for both of them. "No. I think we'll just head on out of here."

"May we give them your phone number?" Wanda wanted to know.

"The baby's parents?" Dillon asked. "Of course. You have a piece of paper?"

Wanda said they'd get the numbers from the statements Dillon and Cat had just given. Dillon made more polite noises. And at last, they were out of there.

They went through the glass doors and Cat felt a moment's relief. But only a moment's, because Rudy Crebs, editor and chief reporter for the *Red Dog City Clarion* was waiting on the steps.

"Dillon. Cat. We gotta talk."

"Not now, Rudy. Give me a call later, okay?" Dillon ushered Cat around the editor.

"Aw, c'mon, you two. This thing with that baby is going to make national news. Give the local paper a break."

Dillon kept walking but spoke over his shoulder. "Later. We promise."

Rudy was still calling to them as they climbed into the Land Cruiser. "When? Give me a time."

Dillon only waved and started the engine.

"How could he have found out so soon?" Cat wondered aloud once they were back on the short stretch of highway that would take them to Barlin Creek Road.

Dillon shrugged. "He's a reporter. They have radar, believe me."

"He said it will be on national news."

Beside her, Dillon grunted. "Could be right. It's a great human interest story, if you think about it."

Cat leaned against the headrest and closed her eyes. "Yes, I suppose so." Dillon, after all, was a famous man. And the baby was a charmer. And the story would have a happy ending, with the little one reunited with her parents at the end.

Cat still held the quilt in her hands. Its soft folds were warm. She knew if she lifted it to her face, she would smell the baby: milky and sweet. That hollowed-out feeling of loss swept through her again.

"Are you all right, Cat?" Dillon's voice was cautious.

She kept her eyes closed and tried to speak evenly. "I'm fine. Just fine."

When they reached the house, he turned off the engine. She opened her eyes and found him smiling at her.

"Home sweet home," he said.

She forced an answering smile for him—and then realized how many things she had to do. And so did he, really.

"You know," she said, "I think you'd probably better go on over to your place and see if everything's all right there—after the storm, I mean."

His smile faded. "What's happening here, Cat?"

"Nothing."

He looked out the windshield at the woodshed, then back at her. "Look. If a pipe's burst or something, I'll only be calling the handywoman. You. You might just as well come with me now."

"No. Please. You should go and check. And I have to go and visit the houses I take care of for the agency."

He leaned closer. "Cat? What is it? What's wrong?"

"Nothing. Really." She lied again. But then she added more honestly, "I just...I'd like a little time to myself, that's all."

Dillon said nothing for a moment. Then he asked, "How much time?"

Cat felt woefully inadequate right then to answer his simple question. The trip to town had shown her too much. She missed the baby. She wanted Dillon. The baby was gone. And Dillon was...he was trying to reach out to her, she could see that. But for some reason, she just couldn't reach back.

"How much time do you need, Cat?" His voice was so reasonable, *too* reasonable. It sounded dangerous. Cat knew she was pushing him. If she wasn't careful, there would be a confrontation. She didn't think she could take that.

"How much time, Cat?"

"I don't know..."

"Well, figure it out by tonight." Now he'd turned brusque. "Because I'm taking you to dinner."

She blinked. "You're what?"

He chuckled then, and she knew that the dangerous moment had passed—this time, anyway. "Don't look so shocked. We're going out to dinner. Don't worry. It's not that big a deal. You sit at a table. Food is set in front of you. You eat it and enjoy the company of your date. That's me."

She opened her mouth to say she couldn't.

But he was smiling at her so tenderly. "Please?"

And she heard herself say, "Okay."

"Great." He pulled her close. His lips, warm and inviting, touched hers. But the kiss was brief. He pulled back. "I'll pick you up at seven-thirty."

A moment later, she was standing on the side porch, holding the quilt in one hand and waving with the other as he backed away down the driveway. Once he was gone, she ducked inside long enough to grab her keys and toss the quilt onto a chair. Then she set off to check on the houses she was responsible for.

Two hours later, she was home again. The first thing she noticed when she walked in the door was how empty the little house seemed. The second thing she noticed was the cradle, still on the floor in the kitchen, near the warmth of the stove.

The sight of it made the tears start to push at the back of her throat. She couldn't take that. So she scooped the thing up along with the quilt she'd carried back from the sheriff's station. She stuck the quilt in the cradle, lugged it upstairs and shoved it back in the crawl space where it belonged.

After that, she took down all the blankets and rags from the clothesline strung under the eaves. The extra blanket sleeper was there. In the rush to get the baby into town, she'd forgotten to put it in the diaper bag. The sight of it almost finished her off. It was all she could do not to rip it off the line and bury her face in it and cry until her tears had soaked it through.

Somehow, she controlled herself. She took the sleeper down and carefully folded it and left it in the stack with the other folded things from the line, on one of the old brass beds upstairs. Later, in a few days, she'd decide whether she was willing to make the effort to return it to the baby's parents.

That handled, she went downstairs, put the frozen things back in the icebox and threw away the melting snow that had kept her refrigerator cold while the power was out.

She noticed that there were messages on her answering machine, which meant the phone was back in working order. But she couldn't bring herself to see who'd called just yet.

Instead she took a shower—a long one that used up all the newly hot water. She'd barely pulled on clean clothes when the phone rang.

She didn't really want to answer it, but she felt she should. She hadn't checked her messages and the line had been down for so long. So she compromised by standing by the phone and waiting to hear who it was.

As she'd secretly feared, it was Adora. "Sis. It's me. I called earlier, when the lines first went back on. No answer. I'm starting to wonder if—"

Cat picked up the phone. "Hi. I'm here."

Adora sighed with relief. "Oh, good. How are you? Are you all right?"

"Of course, I'm fine."

"How can you be so calm?"

"What do you mean?"

"Cat, it's all over town. About you and that poor little baby and Dillon. Everyone's talking."

"Who's everyone?"

"Oh, come on. Lizzie's called me. And Tasha Brinkman. And even old Rudy Crebs was after me to see if I've talked to you and can give him anything for the paper.

They say it'll be on the *news*. You're heroes, is what you are."

"We are?"

"Of course. You saved that darling little girl."

Cat didn't want to think about that darling little girl. She spoke gruffly. "We did what anyone would have done."

Adora fell silent. Then she asked, "Cat? How are you, really? Is everything . . . all right?"

"Everything is fine." Cat wondered how many times she'd said she was fine in the past few hours. She said it once more. "Fine."

"Sure it is." Adora sounded like she was trying to convince herself as much as anyone. She paused, then asked warily, "Do you want me to come over?"

Cat didn't want that. But she knew that she and Adora really needed to talk. "Listen, I—"

Adora didn't let her finish. "Never mind. Now I think about it, it's kind of a bad time."

"But I—"

"Never mind. Really. Hey, I gotta go."

The line went dead before Cat could say another word.

Eleven

At his house, Dillon found nothing amiss. Someone with a snowplow—probably Nestor Brinkman—had cleared his driveway. Inside, nothing had sprung a leak. Everything looked fine. When he checked his messages, Dillon found one that Cat must have left him the first day of the storm.

He played the message back three times, just to hear her asking him so hesitantly to please give her a call and say that he was all right. Hearing it improved his mood, calmed the edgy feeling he'd had since he'd left her at her house.

She wasn't an easy woman. Not in any way. But it was obvious from her voice on the tape that she cared for him—and that had been *before* the three days they'd just spent together.

Things would work out, he told himself as he headed

for the bathroom and the shower he'd been fantasizing about for two days now. He just had to give her time.

Once he'd had his shower, he called the Spotted Owl Restaurant and reserved a secluded table in the back for eight that night. And then as soon as he hung up the phone, it started ringing again.

It seemed, over the next few hours, that he received a call from each and every reporter in the western United States. The story of daredevil Dillon and the woods-woman and dear little baby Alexa was out. Everyone wanted to hear the scoop from Dillon himself.

Out of habit from the old days, Dillon took the first few calls and told them nothing they didn't already know. But then he reminded himself that he didn't have to court the favor of the media anymore; he was out of the daredevil business. And talking to reporters got old fast. Soon enough, he turned off the ringer on his phone and let his machine handle it.

By the time Dillon left to pick up Cat that night, four reporters had showed up on his doorstep and been asked to leave. When Dillon pulled out onto Barlin Creek Road, a van swung in behind him.

Great, he thought grimly. Here he was trying to engi-neer a nice, low-key evening out with the most private woman he'd ever met—and a news van was following him to her house.

As Dillon drove to pick her up, Cat stood in her bath-room, wearing a bra and a pair of underpants. She was studying her chopped-off-looking hair and her rough hands and her scrubbed-clean, unglamorous face in the ancient full-length mirror that was stuck on the back of the door.

Why, she thought glumly, she really wasn't much to look at at all. And she certainly was not a person who could win the heart of one of the handsomest, most charming men she'd ever known.

She was out of her depth with Dillon. She should just face it.

He wanted to take her on a date, but she knew nothing of dates. As he'd guessed from the first, she had never been on a date in her life. She didn't even have a dress to wear—which was the reason she was still standing in the bathroom in her underwear ten minutes before he was due to pick her up. And even if she did own a dress, she'd feel like a complete fool wearing it. She hadn't worn a dress since her father's funeral, and she'd only done that because her mother had insisted.

With a low groan of misery, Cat flung open the bathroom door and strode to the bedroom, where she settled on—what else?—a pair of jeans and a shirt, both new, but neither the least bit feminine. In the back of her closet, she found the tooled leather cowboy boots she'd bought a couple of years ago during a trip to Tahoe. As she pulled them on, she thought, *Whoa, I am really getting fancy here!*

When she was all dressed, she marched back to the bathroom for another gander in the mirror on the back of the door. She looked as flawed as before, only now she was dressed.

There was a knock at the kitchen door.

Oh, no. He was here.

She started to call out that the door was open, but stopped herself. Earlier, reporters had actually pounded on the door. Two of them. She'd sent them both away. But they had been pushy. She wouldn't put it past one of them to walk right in and sit down if she were foolish enough to yell out that the door was unlocked.

There was another knock. Cat tucked in her shirt for the third time, ran her hands down the sides of her hips to smooth away wrinkles that really weren't there and then, at last, went to answer the door.

The sight of him, even after only a few hours, made her heart beat faster. He was dressed pretty much as she was— only he was the *man* on this date, so it made more sense on him. And, of course, he was so *handsome*. More handsome, really, every time she saw him. If that was possible.

"Can I come in?"

She moved back.

He stepped beyond the threshold and pushed the door shut behind him. "I guess I should warn you."

"What?"

"We're not exactly alone."

She stared at him blankly, then realized what he meant. "The reporters?"

He nodded. "There's a news van, just beyond your driveway on the road. And there are a couple of guys in a late-model Chevy, just sitting there, across the road from the van. So it's going to be an adventure, getting out of here."

"You mean, they'll follow us?"

"Yeah. And anytime we get within ten feet of them, they're going to try to get us to talk to them. Our dinner might not be quite as private as I'd hoped."

Cat rubbed her temples and sank into one of the chairs at the table. "Oh, Dillon, I don't know..."

He didn't speak for a moment, then he sighed. "You don't know what?"

She found she couldn't quite look at him.

"What?" he said again.

"I just . . . I don't know if I can handle this."

"Handle what?"

She threw up a hand in a gesture of frustration. "Everything. It's all too much."

"What's all too much?"

"Everything," she said again. "The reporters. The baby . . ."

"What about the baby?"

"I'm never going to see her again."

He thought about that for a moment, then said, "I don't think that has to be true."

She was angry at him suddenly, an irrational anger, she knew. But that didn't stop her from feeling it. She glared at him. "What are you saying? She's gone. That's a fact."

He met her gaze, unmoved. "Cat, there are options here. I think if you get in touch with the parents, then—"

"But that's just it. I don't *want* to do that. I can't stand to do that. To see her. I got too attached to her. I didn't mean for that to happen, but somehow, it did."

"But if you saw her again, and met her parents, then maybe you could start to—"

She didn't want to hear. She cut him off. "No. No, I don't want to see her." Suddenly the other things that were bothering her were pushing to get out. "And that's not all, Dillon. There's so much more."

"What more?"

"It just . . . it can't work. Between you and me. You have to see that. I never asked for this. And I just can't deal with it at all."

"Cat—"

"And what about Adora? There's Adora to consider, too, you know. I still haven't talked with her. How can I go out to dinner with you when I've been such a coward and haven't even told her what's going on between us? It would be so awful for her to have to see us together or to hear about it secondhand. Can't you see that? You have to see . . ."

But he didn't seem to see. Not at all. "Is that everything?"

"Yes—no. Oh, please. I can't go out with you tonight. Please understand."

"Cat." He reached down and took her hand and pulled her to her feet. She went reluctantly. When she stood before him, he wrapped an arm around her and pulled her close.

The feel of him seemed to drain all the tension from her. She leaned her forehead against his chest and spoke into his shirt. "Please, Dillon. I really can't."

He stroked her hair. "Shh. Shh. You can. You'll see." She breathed in the smell of him, the warmth of him.

She looked up at him. "Oh, Dillon . . ."

"Shh." He bent his head and touched her lips with his own. She stiffened a little, trying her best to remember all those reasons why what they had was never going to work out. But with his body pressed to hers and his arms so tight and good around her, it was hard to remember anything at all but how much she wanted to be held by him.

He murmured, "Kiss me, Cat. It will be all right."

And with a low sigh, she found she was doing just that. Kissing him, sliding her hands up his chest to clasp around his neck, arching her body up so that it curved like a bow into his.

With a soft little moan, she parted her lips and felt his tongue delving in. It seemed at that moment that, together, they might conquer anything—even all her deadly doubts and fears.

But then there was a quick rap on the kitchen door. Before Cat could really register the sound, the door was swinging inward. Cat heard a sharp gasp, just as there was a blinding flash of light that flooded the darkness behind Cat's closed eyes. Cat froze. Then slowly, she turned in Dillon's arms and looked toward the door.

Adora stood there, her pretty face frozen in shock. Behind Adora, a man held a camera over his face. The flash exploded with light once again. The photographer lowered the camera and winked at them.

"Thanks, folks," he said.

"What the hell is this?" Dillon growled from behind Cat. He took a step around Cat, toward the photographer, who immediately spun on his heel and dashed out of sight.

Cat forgot about the photographer. All she could think of was Adora. She reached out. "Adora, please, I—"

"No!" Adora cried. "Don't come near me!" And then she was whirling away, too, disappearing as the photographer had into the darkness beyond the porch.

"Adora!" Cat moved to race after her sister.

But Dillon blocked her path. "Let her go."

"You don't understand. I have to stop her."

"No, you don't."

Cat tried to slip around him; he feinted in front of her again. She demanded, "Get out of my way!"

He took her by the shoulders. "She'll be all right."

She tried to shake free of his grasp. "Let me go."

"Look at me." He waited until she did as he commanded. "Leave her alone. Let her deal with it."

But she couldn't do that. She was too guilty to do that. "No, I . . . I betrayed her. She cares for you, and I—"

He was shaking his head. "Neither of us has done anything wrong, Cat. Stop punishing yourself. You're not

Adora's substitute dad anymore. She's a grown woman. And so are you."

It was too much. She couldn't take it anymore. "Don't you tell me who I am!" The sound was loud and ugly. "You just...get out of my way, Dillon McKenna. Get out of my life!"

That did it.

He dropped his hands from her shoulders. His eyes bored into her, seeking something she just didn't have to give. Then he turned, went to the open door and gently swung it shut.

"Do you mean that?"

Her heart was breaking—she could feel it, giving way into a thousand pieces inside her chest. She nodded. "I tried to tell you. You wouldn't listen. I'm just not...cut out for this."

"Oh, yes, you are." He looked so sad. She wondered what was worse, that long, searching look he'd given her a moment ago—or his sadness now.

He went on, "You're afraid, that's all. And you're letting your fear win out. And I'm through begging you, Cat. I told you that first day I kissed you, it takes two."

"But I can't—"

He didn't let her finish. "Right." His voice was cold now, colder than the icicles that dripped from the eaves of the porch outside. "You can't. Go ahead and say it. Say it over and over. Make yourself believe it. You can't be a woman. Your daddy wanted a son. And a son you're going to be."

"No. That's not—"

"True? The hell it isn't." He put his hand on the counter beside him. His fingers gripped the rim, the knuckles turning white. "This is Dillon you're talking to. A hometown boy. *You* know what *I* was back when, and

I know what you were. Not to mention what your father was."

Cat backed up a step. "Stop—"

"Hell, yes. I remember him. A big man. All man. And your pretty, fluttery little mother, looking up at him like he was God. Every time I saw them, your mother was leaning on him. And he *liked* it, don't kid yourself he didn't. He liked being God. He encouraged all his girls to be his narrow little idea of what a woman was, didn't he?"

"No, he—"

Dillon laughed coldly. "Yes, he did. All of his girls but one. Because your mother had failed him. She hadn't given him a son. So he had to *make* himself a son. Out of you. He may have let your mother name you Catherine Desiree, but everyone knew who you *really* were. He wrote it on your cradle. Mitchell, Jr. That was you. The boy he never had. Tough and strong and ready to take charge when Mitchell, Sr., opted out."

"He did *not* opt out!"

"You're shouting, Cat. Who are you trying to convince? Me? Or just yourself?"

"He died. He couldn't help that. It was not his fault."

"For dying, maybe not. But for denying you the right to be your true self—you're damn right, it was his fault."

"He didn't—"

"He did. You *know* he did. And you believed him when he told you a woman couldn't be strong, when he let you know a woman couldn't take charge, couldn't survive without a man around to tell her what to do. And you saw he was right by the way your mother collapsed after he was gone."

"He did the best he could for me."

"Wrong. He did the best he could for *him*. And even though the man's been dead for seventeen years, he still runs your life."

"That's not true."

"Hell, yes, it is. He runs your life every day you don't let yourself be everything that you are. Every day you go on believing that there's some damn law of nature that says a woman can't be strong and tough and in control. He's what's kept you and me apart from the first. And I'm tired of fighting him, Cat. I'm just not going to do it anymore. I'm no damn miracle worker, I'm only a man."

He took in a long breath and looked down at his boots, then back up at her. "I thought the storm and the incredible accident of that baby appearing in the back of my truck could make a difference for us, could force you to see what you and I could have. But it hasn't, not really, not in the long run. You're just . . . locked into this thing too strongly. And I'm a fool to think you'd ever let it go."

"Dillon, I—"

He shook his head. "Uh-uh. Don't say it. It's over, you're right. Goodbye, Cat Beaudine."

Twelve

That was all. He turned and left her.

Cat didn't move for a while after he was gone. Everything he'd said seemed to ricochet off the walls of the room.

But eventually it came to her that she couldn't stand there in the kitchen forever. So she moved, rather jerkily, over to the door. She engaged the lock and switched off the light. Everything went dark.

"That's better," she whispered aloud.

Then, not knowing what else to do, she went to her bedroom and stretched out, fully clothed, on the bed.

She stared at the darkness and waited for the blessed oblivion of sleep. It was a long time coming. And as she waited for it, she kept going over and over what Dillon had said.

And she felt like a shadow—a half a person—because Dillon was right. She was what her father had made her.

But he'd been wrong in blaming her father because her father *had* done the best he could. It had been up to Cat to grow beyond her father's prejudices. And she hadn't grown. She'd told herself she wanted privacy and freedom, but what she'd really wanted was a way to escape rising to the terrifying challenge of being her true self: a woman with a woman's needs and a woman's responsibilities.

As she lay there, the phone started ringing. It seemed, as the hours crawled by, that it never stopped. But then, very late, whoever kept calling finally gave up. There was quiet.

The first sound Cat heard the next morning was someone knocking on the kitchen door.

With a groan, she rolled over and looked at the digital clock on the nightstand. It blinked twelve midnight at her. She had failed to reset it when the power came back on.

The knocking came again. Cat fumbled for her watch. Then she realized she was wearing it—along with the rest of her clothes, including her boots.

Cat looked at the watch, then groaned again. She'd done some serious oversleeping. It was 10:00 a.m. The fires had gone out and the room was an icebox.

And whoever it was—probably one of those blasted reporters—was still beating on her door.

Cat sat up, raked her fingers through her hair, then swung her boots off the side of the bed. She marched to the kitchen and threw open the door, ready to give some hapless reporter a large piece of her mind.

She got as far as opening her mouth when she saw that the "reporter" was a young woman—and she was holding the baby Cat had never thought to see again.

The woman had that dimple in her chin, just like the baby's. She smiled. "Hello, I'm Marian. Marian Todd?"

For a moment, Cat wondered where her voice had gone.

Marian Todd went on smiling. "You're Cat, right?"

"Uh, yes, right."

"Do you think we could come in?" Marian gestured beyond her shoulder with a toss of her head. "There are reporters at the end of the driveway. I warned them not to follow me, but if I stand here for too long, I don't think they'll be able to resist."

That mobilized Cat. She grabbed Marian by the shoulder and pulled her and the baby inside.

The minute the door was closed behind them, the baby started giggling and waving her arms at Cat.

"She remembers you," Marian said. She turned the baby and held her out, so Cat could take her.

Cat's hands were suddenly sweaty. She rubbed them down the sides of her jeans. "It's freezing in here. I'll just get the fire going and make us some coffee."

Marian Todd said nothing for a moment. Then she brought the baby back against her body and agreed that coffee and a warm fire sounded great.

"Have a seat." Cat gestured at the table. Marian sat down with the baby in her lap and Cat bustled around for a few minutes, stoking fires and setting the coffeepot to perk on a burner on the electric half of the stove. After that, she remembered the blanket sleeper and went to get it.

Finally, with the fires blazing, the coffee heating up and the blanket sleeper in the baby's diaper bag where it belonged, there was nothing else to do but sit down opposite the baby's mother and listen to what she had to say.

"We tried to call you."

Cat swallowed. "I'm sure you did. I haven't been answering the phone much." As if to illustrate her statement, the phone in the other room started ringing. Cat shrugged ruefully and made no move to answer it.

Marian nodded. "I imagine it's all been pretty over-whelming for you."

Cat nodded. "*Overwhelming* is a good word for it."

"We called your friend Dillon last night. And we vis-ited him this morning," Marian explained. "He said you were a very private person. That you were having some trouble dealing with all the media attention. So Larry—that's my husband—and I decided that maybe I'd just come to see you alone, with Alexa. I wanted to... I, um..." All at once, Marian's eyes were filling. She had the baby seated on her lap and she was bouncing her a lit-tle, holding on to one of her tiny hands. Marian bit her lip, and managed to go on. "It was an awful time, those three days. And yet, we survived it. And Alexa is just fine. I can't... I just can't tell you. How much I—"

A desperate need came over Cat right then. She had to move, to get out of that chair. She stood. And when she stood, the baby reached for her again.

"*Oo-ga-ga?*"

"She... wants you to hold her," Marian dared to point out in a broken whisper.

Cat rubbed her hands down her sides again. But there was no refusing the eagerness in those plump, waving arms or the wordless plea in those guileless blue eyes. Cat reached out. Marian stood as Cat had done and passed the baby to Cat.

The baby smiled with delight and her tiny hands reached toward Cat's face. Cat turned her and cradled her small, warm form against her breast, then lowered her chin so the baby could touch her.

The baby sighed softly. Cat's chest felt tight. To hold the baby again was everything. It was the impossible. This cuddly, budding scrap of a person seemed at that moment to be all Cat had denied herself. Dolls and dresses and proms and first kisses. A white gown and a ring of gold.

And Dillon, laughing. Dillon, solemnly meeting her eyes. Dillon, knowing her as she hardly knew herself.

"She's glad to see you," Marian said.

"Hello, there," Cat whispered. "How've you been..." And for the first time, in her mind, she accepted the name the little girl's real parents had given her. "...Alexa?" Then she looked up, to find Marian watching her.

"Thank you," Marian said again. "More than you can ever know. More than I can ever say..."

On the stove, the coffee had started perking. Cat reached over and turned the burner down. Then she sat. Marian followed suit.

Marian stayed for an hour. And in that short space of time, Cat found that it made all the difference in letting Alexa go, to see Alexa with Marian, to hold Alexa and know that her life would be full of love.

When they were each on their third cup of coffee, Marian hesitantly suggested that a press conference was slated for the next day, at two in the afternoon in Reno.

"Please, Cat." She leaned across the table, urgent and determined. "We all want to get back to our lives. And I think, to do that, we have to let the media people ask all their questions, and answer them as best we can. If we all show up there—you and Dillon, me, Larry and Alexa, and give them twenty minutes of our time, I think we'll finally be able to go outside our own front doors again without having microphones stuck in our faces."

Cat nodded. She knew that Marian was right, but the idea of voluntarily submitting to the prodding and probing of a roomful of reporters made her want to run for cover.

"Is that nod a yes?" Marian asked hopefully.

Cat took in a deep breath. "I'll think about it, Marian. I promise."

Marian smiled her warm smile. "That's all I can ask."

After Marian left, Cat couldn't sit still. She kept thinking about Adora.

The moment came when she could no longer just hide in her house, listening to the phone ring, wishing the reporters outside would go away. She grabbed her keys and her jacket and went out and got in her pickup. Ignoring the news van and the brown Chevrolet that followed her there, Cat drove to Red Dog City.

Lola Pierce, the other operator in the Shear Elegance Salon of Beauty, looked up from the appointment book when Cat came in the door. "Hey, Adora. You got company."

Adora glanced up and saw Cat. Her full lips pursed. She was in the process of giving Pilar Swenson, who worked in the doughnut shop next door, a blow-dry.

Cat said, above the buzz of the dryer, "Adora. We have to talk."

Adora's lip was quivering. She switched off the dryer. "Pilar?" Her voice was shaky.

"Yes, sweetie?"

"Do you mind if Lola finishes you up?"

"No, hon. That's fine. You go on and have your talk with Cat."

They sat in Adora's living room at either end of her couch.

Cat tried to begin. "Adora, I—"

But then Adora burst out, "Oh, Cat. I didn't sleep all night. It seems like I haven't slept in *days*."

Cat rubbed her eyes. "I know exactly what you mean."

"I've been a total jerk."

"No—"

"Yes. A complete creep. And I *am* sorry. I was going to come and tell you later today, but you beat me to it."

"I did?"

"Hmm-hmm. Oh, this is awful. So hard to say."

"What?"

"I just wouldn't believe him."

"You mean Dillon?"

Adora nodded. "He was straight with me, Cat. He told me it wasn't going to happen between him and me, that he was interested in you. And you know, I think I knew deep in my heart that whatever Dillon and I had had was over sixteen years ago. But I...well, all I kept thinking was that you didn't even *want* a man. And I wanted one so desperately. And not only that, I realized I'd actually *helped* him figure out how to get to know you, by telling him all the things you can do, and suggesting he hire you. I felt like a fool. It just didn't seem fair, you know?"

Cat nodded.

"And I know you," her sister said in tender accusation. "I know what you did. You even tried...to give him up. For my sake. Didn't you?"

"Oh, Adora..."

"Stop." Adora put up her hand. The tears in her eyes welled over and trailed down her cheeks. "Your face says it all. And you can be nice and say you forgive me, but I *was* a total jerk. And then, when I walked in on the two of you last night, it was the moment of truth for me. I knew at last that I was going to have to stop lying to myself about who Dillon really wanted. I was as jealous as they come. And I showed it. I truly am sorry."

Cat reached across the distance between them and smoothed a stray curl of her sister's silky brown hair. "It's forgiven. And forgotten."

"I'm so glad." Adora got up then. When she came back, she had a boxful of tissues in one hand and a bottle of brandy in the other.

"Oh, we shouldn't," Cat said. "It's barely noon."

"I know, but that's not going to stop us. Not on a day like today. Hold on. I'll get the glasses."

A half an hour later, Adora had built up enough courage to ask, "So where *is* he, then? And don't you dare say, 'Who?' "

Cat sipped her brandy and welcomed the trail of fire that burned down her throat to her belly and spread out from there. "I don't know where Dillon is."

Adora shook her head. Her green eyes were wet again. "Oh, Cat. Don't do this. Don't throw love away. After the hateful part I've played in this mess, I'll never forgive myself if you and Dillon don't work things out."

Cat's legs suddenly felt cramped. She stood and stretched, then wandered over to the front window, which looked down on Bridge Street, now blanketed with snow. For a moment, she stared out at the layers of white.

Then she turned back to Adora. "Tomorrow in Reno, there's going to be a press conference. Marian—that's the mother of the baby Dillon found in his truck—has asked me to be there."

Adora blew her nose. "Will *Dillon* be there?"

"Yes, I think so."

"Great." Adora stood. Her pretty chin was set. She radiated determination. "We've got a lot of work to do."

Cat eyed her sister warily. "What kind of work?"

"You've got to look just right for this. I'm telling you, Cat. There are times when a good cut is everything. And take it from an expert. This is one of those times."

* * *

The next day at 1:35, Cat was ushered in a back door of the hall in Reno that had been rented for the press conference.

"Ms. Beaudine?" A woman with a clipboard marched up to her. "I'll take her now," the woman said to the guard who'd let Cat in. She turned to Cat again. "You *are* Ms. Beaudine?"

"Yes." Cat smiled and tried to look self-assured and at ease, as if she wore tailored little suit dresses all the time—not to mention makeup, panty hose and low-heeled pumps.

"You look great," the woman said as she helped Cat out of her coat.

"Why, thank you, I—"

The woman turned to a man walking by. "Ernie. Hang this up for Ms. Beaudine, will you?" Ernie took the coat. The woman whirled back around and spoke to Cat again. "We'll see it's returned to you, after the press conference."

"All right."

Now the woman stepped away and gave Cat a long once-over. "Great," she said again. "Really great. But we were under the impression that you went in for a more rustic look."

"Well, I . . ."

"No, no. It's all right. This is good. This is fine. Now, come on this way. We'll take you somewhere that you can relax until we're ready for you and the others."

Cat wanted to ask how anyone could be expected to relax in the few minutes before they were confronted with a hall full of newspeople. But the woman gave her no chance for questions. She whirled and trotted away, looking very official with her clipboard tucked under her arm. Cat shrugged and followed—to a conference room, with couches and chairs along the walls.

The Todds were already there. Cat introduced herself to Larry Todd, whose smile was every bit as friendly and warm as Marian's. Then she sat down with them to wait.

Dillon appeared a few minutes later, wearing gray slacks and a cable-knit sweater and looking so big and solid and wonderful that Cat was positive all over again that a man such as he could never really be interested in someone like her. He stood in the doorway and made a quick scan of the room.

It seemed as if his gaze burned right through her when it touched her. Cat knew he noticed everything—her new clothes and the haircut Adora had labored over for hours, not to mention the eye makeup and lipstick she was wearing. She felt like a fool. She wanted to get up and run out of there. And she wanted to hurl herself at him, throw her arms around his neck and beg him to give her just one more chance.

She did neither. The moment passed. Dillon strode toward them, a cordial smile on his face.

Larry Todd stood. "Dillon." The men shook hands.

Alexa, in Marian's arms, was making eager noises and waving her plump hands. Marian held the baby up.

Dillon took her and swung her in the air. "How're you doing? How's the girl?"

Alexa laughed merrily. Then Dillon sat, on the other side of Larry, and put Alexa in his lap. *"Oog-wa,"* Alexa said, looking very pleased with herself. The little bow Marian had tied around her head was slightly askew. Marian reached out and set it straight.

For a few more minutes, they sat and talked quietly. Cat tried not to stare at Dillon, though since the moment he'd entered the room, she'd been aware of little else but him. The air seemed to vibrate with his special, warm energy.

And every time he spoke, her nerve endings quivered in silent response.

At last, the woman with the clipboard reappeared. "If you will all come this way now."

She led them to a backstage area, then through the wings, in front of the curtains and onto the stage where there were two folding tables and several chairs set up, with microphones waiting at each chair. There was already a man sitting at one of the microphones.

"Darah Rankin's psychiatrist," Marian whispered, in response to a questioning look from Cat.

The woman with the clipboard showed Cat which chair to sit in. Obediently Cat took her seat. Dillon was led to the chair on her right, and Marian, holding Alexa, to her left. On the other side of Marian was Larry and to Larry's left was the man Marian had said was a psychiatrist.

Cat was very careful, for those first few seconds, not to look directly out into the auditorium. She knew that the rows of folding chairs were full, and that there were video cameras and all kinds of photographic equipment everywhere. Flashbulbs kept going off, explosions of light that blinded Cat each time she looked up.

A man in a blue suit introduced them all and requested that no photos be taken during the question-and-answer period. The psychiatrist, a Dr. Poole, came under scrutiny first. He had a little speech prepared.

"Mrs. Rankin," he said of the woman who had abducted Alexa, "is a very ill woman. She is currently under strict psychiatric supervision in a place where she will be sure to get all the care she so desperately needs."

One of the reporters stood. "Have any charges been filed against her?"

Larry spoke up. "Not by us. We understand that Mrs. Rankin has suffered greatly, and we will be satisfied if she is able to get the help Dr. Poole just described."

The man in the blue suit added, "I'm afraid charges of child endangerment and kidnapping will be filed by the state of Nevada. But a judge will decide whether or not Mrs. Rankin could have been considered responsible for her actions at the time of the abduction."

A woman stood. "Mr. McKenna, our sources tell us that you've been inspired by this whole incident to jump a certain ravine up by Mount Shasta on a specially built jet bike."

Dillon rubbed his temple with the fingers of his left hand. "Would your *sources* include a Mr. L. W. Creedy, by any chance?"

"I can't divulge that information."

"Well, whoever your sources are, you've been misinformed. I'm out of the daredevil business. And even a beautiful baby like little Alexa here hasn't changed my mind about that."

Someone else popped up. "Mrs. Todd, how does it feel to have your baby back?"

"Indescribable, the greatest gift I've ever received."

"Ms. Beaudine, did you grow attached to that little girl?"

Cat cleared her throat, which had closed up the moment the reporter said her name. Somehow she managed to get out, "Did I ever." Her voice came out tight, with a little squeak at the end.

A ripple of laughter rolled over the hall, but it was friendly laughter. Cat felt that the reporters were on her side. She breathed a little easier. This wasn't as bad as she'd expected.

After that, the questions came fast and furious. In the course of the next twenty minutes, Dillon and Cat and the Todds were asked to detail all that they'd gone through during the worst blizzard in more than a decade. There was so much to tell about everything else, Cat actually allowed herself to hope that the question of herself and Dillon and what *they* might have shared during those three days wouldn't come up.

But no such luck. The question was not to be avoided.

A tall woman with a strident voice spoke up. "Rumor has it that romance has bloomed between you and Ms. Beaudine, Mr. McKenna. Care to comment on that?"

Dillon's smile froze on his face. He leaned toward his microphone. "No," he said very clearly.

Someone held up a tabloid newspaper. On the front page was one of the two stolen shots of Dillon and Cat in her kitchen—the first one, when they'd been locked in a torrid embrace.

"Comment on *this*, Mr. McKenna," the man with the tabloid said with a smirk.

Dillon was no longer making even an attempt to smile. "As I said before, I have no comment. There is nothing going on between Ms. Beaudine and me."

"If that's nothing—" the man with the tabloid in his hand leered "—I'd love to see *something*."

There was whispering and some laughter—more salacious than friendly now.

"All right, everybody," the man in the blue suit cut in. "Any other questions?"

Cat leaned toward her microphone. "Um . . ."

The room fell silent. It was eerie. All Cat had done was make that one little sound, and everyone was listening.

She took in a breath that sounded like a gale-force wind, amplified as it was. And then she said, "I would like to say something about that, about me and Mr. McKenna."

The packed room was so quiet by then it seemed possible to hear the snow melting outside. Cat could feel hundreds of eyes, watching, waiting. But all the staring eyes meant nothing—only one pair of eyes mattered. Dillon's. And she couldn't bring herself to turn her head right then and see if he was staring, too.

Cat sucked in another gale-force breath—which made the mike pop when she released it.

And then she said, right into the microphone, for all the world to hear, "I'm in love with Dillon McKenna."

There was a silence so deafening, Cat thought her eardrums would burst.

And then out of the silence, Alexa Todd crowed in delight.

After that it was pandemonium.

"Mr. McKenna! Mr. McKenna!" One reporter's voice rose above the rest. "What do you have to say to that?"

Dillon said something crude under his breath.

"Could you repeat that?" the reporter demanded. "We didn't quite hear it."

"This is private," Dillon growled. And Cat, who still hadn't dared to really look at him, felt his hand close over hers. She blinked and looked up at him as he stood up so fast that he bumped the table, jarring the microphones, which promptly made the speakers around the room scream in a frenzy of feedback.

"Come on," he commanded beneath the electronic whine. "We're getting out of here." He yanked on her hand.

Cat cleared her throat. "But don't you think we ought to—"

"I mean it. Come on." He pulled her to her feet.

She didn't know what made her do it, but in the seconds before he towed her out of there, she bent to speak into her microphone once more. "We'll keep you posted...."

"Come *on*, Cat." And then he was striding for the wings. Cat followed, partly because he was dragging her along and partly because she would have followed him anywhere.

The lady with the clipboard tried to stop them. "Really, people, this is highly irregular."

Dillon just stepped around her, holding tightly to Cat's hand. He started to run.

With the sounds of the shouting from the hall fading behind them, they fled down a corridor, past the conference room where they'd waited earlier and then down another hallway to the back door where Cat had come in.

"Dillon," Cat said then. "My coat. I left my—"

"Forget the damn coat," he barked over his shoulder. "I'll buy you a thousand coats. We're getting the hell out of here."

Dillon pushed the bar handle and shoved back the door.

"Er, goodbye now, Mr. McKenna, Ms. Beaudine," said the security guard standing right outside.

Cat managed to wave at the man, before Dillon dragged her away across the dirty, frozen snow of the parking lot.

"Get in," he commanded, as he unlocked the passenger door of a low, metallic-blue sports car that Cat had never seen before.

"But where's your Land Cruiser?"

He shrugged. "I was depressed yesterday, so I bought a Maserati."

"Oh. Right. Of course. I hope it helped."

"It didn't. Get in."

Cat obeyed, because it was exactly what she wanted to do. Dillon was behind the wheel. He started the powerful engine. The car roared in readiness just as reporters started pouring out of the back door of the hall.

Dillon swung out of the parking space. The tires slid on the hard-packed snow. Dillon gave the wheel its way for a moment, until the tires found purchase again. Then he aimed the low nose of the car at the street. When he reached it, he spun the wheel to the left and hit the gas.

"Dillon, be careful!" Cat screeched, locking her seat belt in place.

He shot her a grin. "Relax. I used to do this for a living, remember?"

He turned the corner without hitting the brakes. Cat held on to the armrest and waited to die.

But she didn't die. An hour later, they were checked into a suite on the top floor of one of Reno's best casino/hotels. Dillon engaged the privacy lock and turned to look at her.

What she saw on his face caused that womanly feeling of weakness all through her. She welcomed the feeling.

She backed away, through the little entryway, into the sitting room of the suite. Dillon matched every step that she took.

"The desk clerk did a double take the moment he saw your face."

He shrugged. "Breaks of the game."

"There'll be reporters camped outside the door of the suite within a half hour."

"So what? Weren't you the one who said we'd keep them posted?"

"I'm not sure. It all happened so fast." The backs of her knees met one of the plush, heavily padded easy chairs in the sitting room. She dropped into the chair.

"Don't play innocent now. I know what you said." Dillon kept coming until he stood right over her, that bone-melting look still in his eyes.

She crossed her legs, feeling the nylon of the panty hose slide seductively against her skin. "It wasn't so bad, talking to reporters, once I relaxed a little."

His lips hinted at a smile. "You relaxed a *lot,* I would say."

"Oh, would you?"

"Who cut your hair?"

"Adora."

"And the little business suit and the makeup?"

"All Adora. We worked out all our problems and then she gave me a few pointers. She has excellent taste."

"You look great." He sounded grim.

"Thank you."

"Did you mean what you said back there? And if you say 'What?' I'm going to wrap my hands around your pretty neck and strangle you."

"I meant it."

"Then say it again—only to me. Say it right to me."

"I love you, Dillon."

He was quiet. Then he took her hand and slowly pulled her to her feet. He started unbuttoning the tailored jacket that went over her slim, fitted wool dress. "I like the way you look in this. But I like you in your old jeans and boots, too."

"I'm glad."

"And I like you naked best of all." He slid the jacket off her shoulders and tossed it on the chair, then he turned her around and slowly unzipped the dress. With a caressing stroke of each hand, he pushed the dress off her shoulders so it fell at her feet. She cavalierly kicked it away and then stepped out of her shoes as well.

All she had on then were her panty hose and the little camisole and tap pants that Adora had made her buy. She wore no bra.

Dillon let out a shaky breath. "I love you, too."

Cat smiled. Slowly she gathered up the hem of his sweater and guided it over her belly and chest, then off his raised arms. "I think I knew it. But I love to hear it."

"Should I say it again?"

She touched his chest, spreading her fingers in the mat of hair there. "Yes. Tell me again." She moved closer to him, sliding her hands around his neck, resting her head against his heart. "Tell me forever."

His arms closed around her. "I will. If you'll marry me."

"Yes, Dillon. Oh, yes."

He scooped her up then, against his chest, and he carried her to the huge bed in the other room.

And then she realized what she'd forgotten. "Dillon. I didn't bring anything. No little foil packets."

He laid her down and stretched out beside her, then lazily guided a satin strap from her shoulder and planted a kiss there. "We did all right with Alexa."

She pushed his chest a little, until he met her eyes. "What are you saying?"

"I'm saying we could probably handle a baby of our own. The truth is, I've got all kinds of plans for the kind of life we'll lead."

She stroked his hair back from his forehead with her fingers. "Tell me those plans. Please?"

He kissed the tip of her nose, and then reached under the hem of the camisole, seeking the soft mound of her breast. She sighed when he found it.

He chuckled and rubbed her nipple with his thumb.

"Tell me," she said again, only huskier than before.

"All right. I want you to go to college, the way you should have, all those years ago. I want you to get that engineering degree."

"Oh, Dillon."

"And I want us to have babies. I want to raise babies. Ours. And maybe other children, too, children that will become ours, we'll love them so much."

"You mean adopt?"

He nodded. "I had such a lousy childhood, I'd like to give some kids who really need it a chance. Would that bother you? Adopting a kid or two?"

"I don't know. I never thought about it."

"We could work together on it. Like we did with Alexa."

She found she was laughing through the tears in her eyes. "It's crazy."

"What's crazy?"

"I thought I was such a private person. And that my freedom was the most important thing in my life. But now, since you came along, I'm announcing that I love you to a roomful of reporters. And thinking that it would be a great idea to get an engineering degree and raise a houseful of kids."

Under the camisole, his hand moved. Cat sighed and lifted her arms to pull him down to her.

"We're gonna make it, Cat. We're gonna have a great life," he whispered as his mouth met hers.

She said nothing. No words were needed. Since Dillon McKenna had returned to Red Dog City, the world had become a place where anything could happen. A place where even solitary, mannish Cat Beaudine might find all the love and happiness that once had passed her by.

*   *   *   *   *

SILHOUETTE® Desire®

COMING NEXT MONTH

#943 THE WILDE BUNCH—Barbara Boswell
August's *Man of the Month*, rancher Mac Wilde, needed a woman to help raise his four kids. So he took Kara Kirby as his wife in name only....

#944 COWBOYS DON'T QUIT—Anne McAllister
Code of the West
Sexy cowboy Luke Tanner was trying to escape his past, and Jillian Crane was the only woman who could help him. Unfortunately, she also happened to be the woman he was running from....

#945 HEART OF THE HUNTER—BJ James
Men of the Black Watch
Fifteen years ago, Jeb Tanner had mysteriously disappeared from Nicole Callison's life. Now the irresistible man had somehow found her, but how could Nicole be sure his motives for returning were honorable?

#946 MAN OVERBOARD—Karen Leabo
Private investigator Harrison Powell knew beautiful Paige Stovall was hiding something. But it was too late—she had already pushed him overboard...with desire!

#947 THE RANCHER AND THE REDHEAD—Susannah Davis
The only way Sam Preston could keep custody of his baby cousin was to marry. So he hoodwinked Roni Daniels into becoming his wife!

#948 TEXAS TEMPTATION—Barbara McCauley
Hearts of Stone
Jared Stone was everything Annie Bailey had ever wanted in a man, but he was the one man she could *never* have. Would she risk the temptation of loving him when everything she cared about was at stake?

MILLION DOLLAR SWEEPSTAKES (III)

No purchase necessary. To enter, follow the directions published. Method of entry may vary. For eligibility, entries must be received no later than March 31, 1996. No liability is assumed for printing errors, lost, late or misdirected entries. Odds of winning are determined by the number of eligible entries distributed and received. Prizewinners will be determined no later than June 30, 1996.

Sweepstakes open to residents of the U.S. (except Puerto Rico), Canada, Europe and Taiwan who are 18 years of age or older. All applicable laws and regulations apply. Sweepstakes offer void wherever prohibited by law. Values of all prizes are in U.S. currency. This sweepstakes is presented by Torstar Corp., its subsidiaries and affiliates, in conjunction with book, merchandise and/or product offerings. For a copy of the Official Rules send a self-addressed, stamped envelope (WA residents need not affix return postage) to: MILLION DOLLAR SWEEPSTAKES (III) Rules, P.O. Box 4573, Blair, NE 68009, USA.

EXTRA BONUS PRIZE DRAWING

No purchase necessary. The Extra Bonus Prize will be awarded in a random drawing to be conducted no later than 5/30/96 from among all entries received. To qualify, entries must be received by 3/31/96 and comply with published directions. Drawing open to residents of the U.S. (except Puerto Rico), Canada, Europe and Taiwan who are 18 years of age or older. All applicable laws and regulations apply; offer void wherever prohibited by law. Odds of winning are dependent upon number of eligibile entries received. Prize is valued in U.S. currency. The offer is presented by Torstar Corp., its subsidiaries and affiliates in conjunction with book, merchandise and/or product offering. For a copy of the Official Rules governing this sweepstakes, send a self-addressed, stamped envelope (WA residents need not affix return postage) to: Extra Bonus Prize Drawing Rules, P.O. Box 4590, Blair, NE 68009, USA.

SWP-S795

He's Too Hot To Handle...but she can take a little heat.

SILHOUETTE

Summer Sizzlers

This summer don't be left in the cold, join Silhouette for the hottest Summer Sizzlers collection. The perfect summer read, on the beach or while vacationing, Summer Sizzlers features sexy heroes who are "Too Hot To Handle." This collection of three new stories is written by bestselling authors Mary Lynn Baxter, Ann Major and Laura Parker.

Available this July wherever Silhouette books are sold.

SS95

As a Privileged Woman,
you'll be entitled to all these Free Benefits.
And Free Gifts, too.

To thank you for buying our books, we've designed an exclusive FREE program called *PAGES & PRIVILEGES™*. You can enroll with just one Proof of Purchase, and get the kind of luxuries that, until now, you could only read about.

BIG HOTEL DISCOUNTS

A privileged woman stays in the finest hotels. And so can you—at up to 60% off! Imagine standing in a hotel check-in line and watching as the guest in front of you pays $150 for the same room that's only costing you $60. Your *Pages & Privileges* discounts are good at Sheraton, Marriott, Best Western, Hyatt and thousands of other fine hotels all over the U.S., Canada and Europe.

FREE DISCOUNT TRAVEL SERVICE

A privileged woman is always jetting to romantic places. When <u>you</u> fly, just make one phone call for the lowest published airfare at time of booking—<u>or double the difference back!</u> PLUS—you'll get a $25 voucher to use the first time you book a flight AND <u>5% cash back on every ticket you buy thereafter through the travel service!</u>

SD-PP3A

FREE GIFTS!

A privileged woman is always getting wonderful gifts.
Luxuriate in rich fragrances that will stir your senses (and his). This gift-boxed assortment of fine perfumes includes three popular scents, each in a beautiful designer bottle. <u>Truly Lace</u>...This luxurious fragrance unveils your sensuous side. <u>L'Effleur</u>...discover the romance of the Victorian era with this soft floral. <u>Muguet des bois</u>...a single note floral of singular beauty.

FREE INSIDER TIPS LETTER

A privileged woman is always informed. And you'll be, too, with our free letter full of fascinating information and sneak previews of upcoming books.

MORE GREAT GIFTS & BENEFITS TO COME

A privileged woman always has a lot to look forward to. And so will you. You get all these wonderful FREE gifts and benefits now with only one purchase...and there are no additional purchases required. However, each additional retail purchase of Harlequin and Silhouette books brings you a step closer to even more great FREE benefits like half-price movie tickets... and even more FREE gifts.

L'Effleur...This basketful of romance lets you discover L'Effleur from head to toe, heart to home.

Truly Lace...
A basket spun with the sensuous luxuries of Truly Lace, including Dusting Powder in a reusable satin and lace covered box.

Complete the Enrollment Form in the front of this book and mail it with this Proof of Purchase.

PROOF OF PURCHASE
Offer expires October 31, 1996

SD-PP3